JUSTICE RIDES AGAIN

JOHN DEACON

Cover design by German Creative on Fiverr

Edited by Karen Bennett

Want to know when my next book is released? SIGN UP HERE.

❀ Created with Vellum

CHAPTER 1

The tall man was hidden behind his paper as Susan approached with a carafe of steaming coffee.

And that, Susan thought, was a shame. He wasn't just handsome. He radiated an almost savage intensity, which was odd because he was so calm and polite.

How was that even possible?

Susan stifled a laugh and shook her head. She'd always been a dreamer, had always been plagued by the strangest notions, but this one—oh, Susan—this one pretty much took the cake.

"Warm you up, sir?" she said, reaching his table.

The man lowered the paper, a slight smile coming onto his scarred, square-jawed face.

"Yes, please."

Meeting his gaze for an instant, Susan nearly shuddered.

Those eyes.

They were deep green. Not the green of emeralds or clover. A deeper green, the green of a misty forest from the depths of time, when men with wits as sharp as arrowheads hunted living meat with clubs and spears.

What has gotten into you, Susan? she wondered, filling the man's coffee again.

"Thank you very much, ma'am," the man said, his voice soft yet husky.

"You're welcome, sir. Is there anything else I can get for you?"

"No thank you, ma'am. This sure did hit the spot."

"Well, I'm glad to hear that, sir. You just take your time, and I'll keep the coffee coming."

She carried the coffee to another table and refilled the cups of a tired-looking man and his sour-faced wife and listened as the woman complained about her eggs.

Susan told the woman she would take the eggs back to the cook and bring out another plate.

"I won't pay extra."

"No, ma'am. We'll replace the eggs free of charge."

"Good, because I won't pay extra."

On her way back to the kitchen, Susan saw the man had returned his attention to the front page of the newspaper. His striking green eyes flicked back and forth across the print with fierce focus as if he were committing every line to memory.

By the time she came back out of the kitchen with another plate of eggs for the sour-faced woman, she felt a little sour herself, seeing the man heading for the door.

Then, glancing at his table, she saw a five-dollar gold piece sitting atop the folded newspaper.

Instantly, she feared he'd made a mistake, accidentally leaving far too much money; but just as instantly, she understood he hadn't. This was a man who never made mistakes, a singular man, the sort of man we're lucky to meet once in our lives.

He'd just given her the tip of a lifetime, an extra week's salary that would ease her present worries a good deal.

"Thank you so much, sir," she called after him, but the door had already closed behind him.

Susan stood there for a moment, watching him cross the street to the train station. He was very tall with broad shoulders and narrow hips upon which hung two pistols. Despite his great height, he moved with all the muscular grace of a mountain lion as he swung open the station door and held it for a pair of elderly women who tottered in before him.

Then, he followed after them, the train station door closed, and Susan felt an absurd sense of loss.

She laughed at herself. *You can't lose what you never had.*

"Are you bringing me those eggs or waiting for them to get cold?" the sour-faced woman called.

"Sorry, ma'am," Susan said, wishing there was some way to put people like this miserable woman in her place.

"It's about time," the woman said, frowning at the new plate of eggs.

The tired-looking man offered Susan a sympathetic smile. The poor man. Susan couldn't imagine dealing with such a woman day after day, year after year.

His irritable wife sighed dramatically, poking the eggs with her fork. "I guess these will have to do."

Feeling a wave of uncharacteristic boldness, Susan said, "If you don't like the eggs, go to the restaurant down the street and complain about their food."

The woman blinked at her, gaping.

Susan braced herself for an angry tirade.

Instead, the woman's sour face went pink, and she dropped her eyes and went to work on her breakfast without further complaint.

Susan turned, feeling a surge of joy. What had gotten into her? What in the world had given her the audacity to challenge that woman?

And then she knew.

The man.

She had taken strength from her brief encounter with the mysterious man, some part of her understanding he would never stand for the petty bullying of the egg-rejecting shrew.

Susan smiled as she cleared his table, but her smile faded as she saw the headline in the paper he'd been reading.

THE WILD WILLIAMS BROTHERS KILL AGAIN!

Her eyes scanned the first few lines with a chill, reading about the frightening outlaws terrorizing Cedar Fork.

She closed the newspaper with a shudder and again stared out the window toward the train station.

She sure hoped the tall man wasn't going anywhere near Cedar Fork. She hated to think of him running into ruthless killers like Preston and Carter Williams and couldn't even bear to think of anything happening to such a good, kind man like him.

But she was being silly again, of course. The man had read the paper, after all, and he seemed intelligent and sensible.

Surely, he would know enough to steer clear of such a place and such men.

———

PRESTON WILLIAMS DROWNED ON HIS OWN BLOOD, LYING ON THE dirt floor of his hideout with his own Bowie buried in his chest.

Ten feet away, Carter Williams swung the axe once more—and missed again.

Justice swept into the weapon's wake, jammed his own fighting knife into Williams's solar plexus.

Williams squealed and went rigid.

Justice slipped behind the murderer, grabbed his long hair, gave a mighty tug, and threw Williams to the floor.

An instant later, Justice's Colt was in his hand. "You and your brother will never rape or murder again."

Carter Williams coughed blood, clutching the hilt of the knife buried in his body, and glared up at Justice, his eyes burning with hatred and confusion. "Who are you? How did you find us?"

"I'm Justice," he said, raising the Colt, "and I always find you."

"Always? I never seen you before in my—"

The Colt boomed. A red hole appeared between Williams's eyes, and one more killer had fallen silent forever.

Justice had been served.

CHAPTER 2

As Justice neared home, he saw his closest neighbor and good friend, Diego Contreras, riding his way.

"Just the man I was hoping to see," Diego said, bringing his bay close. "Welcome home."

They shook and rode together toward Justice's ranch.

"What brings you off the homestead, Diego? Cattleman association business?"

"No, everything's good there. You'd never think all these hard-nosed ranchers could get along like a bunch of church ladies at a chicken dinner, but they do."

Justice nodded. "We fought together, fought for this valley. These men appreciate what they've got and respect each other. I reckon when those two things are in place, folks get along just fine."

"I suppose that is correct, my friend."

They came around the final curve, and Justice's heart warmed, as it always did, to see his home. Thanks to Nora and a lot of hard work, it was a neat and tidy ranch, bright with new grass and spring flowers.

Over recent weeks, they'd added a second bunkhouse and nearly finished a large guesthouse as well, realizing with Justice gone so much of the time, they could use more help around the place; not just cowpokes but farm hands as well, and a full-time cook, whom they had not yet hired but who would live and cook in the guesthouse, which would also see frequent use, they hoped, by family members such as Matt, newlyweds Luke and Faith, and Nora's mother and other sisters and their families.

"So, if you're not here on cattleman business, what did you want to talk about?"

"Wolves."

"Wolves?"

Diego nodded. "And dogs," he added with a grin. "And half-wolves."

"What are you talking about?"

"You remember me saying my best dog, Consuela, was pregnant?"

"Oh yeah. Last time I was over, you kept complaining because she was the only dog who could control that mean bull of yours."

Diego nodded. "She's gonna have a time with him when she gets back out there. He's gotten cocky in her absence."

"Wouldn't be a bull if he didn't."

"Consuela had her puppies. But they don't look like border collies. They look like wolves."

Justice laughed. "You think some wolf came down out of the mountains and had his way with her?"

Diego shook his head. "Consuela's tougher than a boar hog.

No beast could have his way with Consuela unless she invited him. It wasn't a wolf."

At that moment, a shaggy, many-colored creature with a lolling tongue trotted out of the scrub to greet Justice, who suddenly understood.

"Oh."

"Yes, oh," Diego said. "Looks like our dogs have joined houses, so to speak."

"Well, they'll be strong pups."

Diego nodded. "They are. It's a small litter of big pups. I'm keeping the two females. I'm partial to female dogs, and these two are just ugly enough that they might make good cattle dogs. You can come get the two males in a few weeks."

"I need two puppies like I need a hole in my head."

"My sentiments exactly."

Rafer trotted proudly alongside them, head held high, as they drew closer to the ranch house.

"All right. I'll come out and get them when they're ready. But with two puppies around, Nora's gonna have a time keeping Eli on top of his chores."

"Oh, I'm sure she'll manage. Eli won't be any tougher to wrangle than that bull's been. Speaking of your children, there's Katie hanging out the wash yonder."

Justice's heart sang to see his adopted daughter out by the clothesline, doing her part as always. How he loved that girl. He was so grateful that he'd managed to save her from her uncle in New York City and knew she was happier than she'd ever dreamed she could be.

Katie hadn't seen him yet. He couldn't wait to see her face

when she finally did. There is no purer joy in this world than coming home and seeing the beaming faces of your children.

"She's becoming a woman," Diego said.

"Don't remind me." The girl had filled out over the winter, thanks to good food, hard work, and life among a loving family. She was no longer the skinny orphan he'd rescued. Now, turning and seeing him, Katie smiled brightly and waved and called into the house, looking exactly like what she was: a sixteen-year-old girl of remarkable beauty with a pure heart full of love for her family.

"Hi, Pa!" she called, dropping her laundry into the basket and hurrying forward to meet him. "Hi, Mr. Contreras!"

"You ready for what comes next?" Diego said.

"What's that?"

"You might recall I'm a man with daughters."

Justice nodded.

"What comes next," Diego told him, "is suitors."

"Suitors?" Justice said. "Don't be crazy. She's just a girl."

"You keep telling yourself that, my friend," Diego said, clapping him on the shoulder. "But keep an eye out for wolves. They come sniffing around when you least expect it."

CHAPTER 3

"Well," Justice laughed, breathing hard later that night as Nora, also struggling to catch her breath, snuggled into him, "guess I don't need to ask if you missed me."

Laughing, she smoothed a hand over his chest, absentmindedly tracing the star-shaped scar where a badge had once been melted into his flesh. The silver star had been shot away in his fight against his father's murderer, Oliver Rose, but a five-pointed scar remained, the indelible mark of justice stamped eternally upon him.

"I always miss you, Justice. You are my heart."

"And you're mine, Nora."

"But all the same, I'm glad you're out in the world again. Oh, some nights I get to missing you and feel sorry for myself, but then I think of all those people you're helping and all the people you're saving, folks who will never know that, if you hadn't come along when you did, the men you stop would have shown up at their doorstep and done evil to them as well. Lives lost, families destroyed, hope and dreams stolen forever. You are doing the Lord's work, husband."

"It gets downright bloody at times."

"As did the Lord's work when Elijah slaughtered the priests of Baal."

"Well, I pray the good Lord will give me the wisdom to sort out right from wrong."

"A wise prayer."

For a moment, they just lay together, each loving the feel of the other.

"You find a cook yet?" Justice asked.

Nora shook her head. "I haven't been trying too hard. Katie and I are managing fine. You know how she loves the kitchen."

He grinned at that. "She'll probably throw a fit when you do hire someone to cook."

"I guarantee she'll want to help whomever I hire. She loves to cook almost as much as she loves to read. Maybe even more."

"Now that's saying something." Once again, Justice had come home with a book for his daughter. This time it was *Pinocchio*, the story of a wooden boy who comes to life and causes all sorts of mischief.

When he'd given it to her, she'd lit up light Christmas morning... as had Eli when Justice had handed him the new deck of cards. Somewhat to Nora's chagrin, her son was becoming quite the poker player.

"I do want to find someone," Nora said. "Ever since you suggested the idea, I keep thinking how nice it would be to go visit Mother and my sisters from time to time. But I don't want to rush it, you know? Bringing on hands is one thing. Bringing another woman onto the ranch is quite another."

Justice held up his hands. "That's your domain."

"Yes, it is. I figure the good Lord will make it clear enough when I meet the right person so long as I don't get in His way by trying too hard to find her."

"Well, by the time you find her, the guesthouse should be ready. Did Zimmermann say when he'd finish up?"

"He expects to have everything finished by the end of the week. His crew works quickly."

"They do. And they do good work."

"Which is why they're so expensive."

Justice nodded. He never minded paying more for good work, especially when it was delivered in a timely fashion.

Folks said money was the root of all evil, and that was mostly true. It sure did stir up the worst in some people.

They also said money couldn't buy happiness. Justice supposed that was true, too. At least partially.

Money couldn't buy complete happiness. Even millionaires can be miserable.

But as anyone who's gone without can tell you, money does solve problems; and if you keep your head about you, money can indeed usher a lot of happiness into your life.

The key to happiness, of course, is being thankful for whatever you have.

But it was nice not to have to worry or cut corners, nice to be able to hire good help from folks who took pride in their work. That went for carpenters and cowhands and, he supposed, cooks as well, which underscored Nora's wisdom in waiting for the right woman.

They talked for a while longer about the ranch, Nora saying she thought maybe they could use another ranch hand, too, because Castaneda had wrenched his shoulder and wouldn't be able to do much for a while.

"I've been thinking we could use another hand, anyway," Justice said. "The herd's growing, and you never know when a cowboy might up and leave us. They're drifters at heart."

They talked of the herd and the crops and the height of the river and then Justice remembered Diego's news and told Nora about the pups.

"Puppies?" Nora said, sitting up, suddenly awake. "I'm going to have a time getting Eli to do his work."

"I'll say something to him."

"Would you? If you say something, he'll listen."

"Last I checked, he listened awful good to his mama, too."

"Oh yes, Eli is a good boy. Just as good of a boy as has ever raced across God's green Earth. But you, sir, clearly underestimate the power of puppies."

CHAPTER 4

"Jasper Falco," Sheriff Pat Perkins said, holding up the wanted poster.

A sullen face with a slack jaw and an eye patch stared out at him.

"Looks mean as a bull in breeding season, don't he?" Sheriff Perkins said.

"Most of them do until you shoot them. Then they just look dead."

Perkins gave him a funny smile. "You know, you're a little spooky sometimes, Justice."

"No man need fear me except those who have it coming. And then there's no use being scared because it won't do them any good."

"See, now that's just downright creepy."

"What did Mr. Falco do to earn his way onto that wanted poster?"

"Here, you can read it for yourself." Perkins handed it to him. "Go ahead and keep it if you're going back on the trail."

Justice's eyes flicked over the print. "Cattle rustling? Come on, Perkins. You're the sheriff, not me. You know I don't chase thieves."

Perkins grinned, obviously proud of his little trick. "Well, you clearly neglected to read the telegram that came in one day after the poster. Falco unloaded the cattle and headed north. Sheriff's deputy up in Taos tried to stop him, and Falco plugged him in the belly."

"All right."

"I guess Falco liked killing, because later that night, he stopped by a saloon and killed the bartender. Witnesses said the bartender didn't even do anything. Falco ordered a bottle of whiskey, the bartender got it, and Falco shot him through the heart. Turned to the people, said he didn't pay nobody for nothing and if anybody was feeling lucky to just go ahead and slap leather and the others could bury them next to the barkeep."

Justice shook his head. "Another killer in need of killing."

"When are you going hunting?"

"Soon. Probably in the morning. You got anything else for me?"

"Not at the moment, but given the state of the world today, I'm sure fresh trouble will show up soon."

CHAPTER 5

Cyrus Undergrove rode into Plank City beneath a blistering midday sun. A short, broad-shouldered man, he rode slowly, savoring the moment. The cigar stub clamped in his feral grin smoldered as Cyrus turned his sweating, unshaven face from side to side, watching the skittish townsfolk notice this crew of rough, hard-looking strangers.

Behind Undergrove rode eight of his nine men.

Reaching the bank, Cyrus glanced across the street and saw the wink of metal in sunlight. His final man, former buffalo hunter Hank Hardesty, was up there with his Sharps.

The men dismounted and tethered their horses loosely to the hitching post in front of the bank.

They didn't have to talk. Cyrus had drilled the procedure into their heads over and over, and they'd already pulled two successful jobs together.

A moment later, they went through the door. Cyrus entered first, pulling a Colt and aiming at a startled man, who dropped a fistful of greenbacks and threw his hands in the air with a yelp.

"We have come here to relieve you of your money," Cyrus announced.

Frightened women cried out.

Three customers waited before two male tellers. Two of these customers were women, one old crone and one younger, attractive woman.

The third customer was a wiry, middle-aged man in dungarees, a bright white shirt, and a nice, white Stetson that looked like it had just come off the rack.

The man might've been dressed like some kind of gentleman rancher, but Cyrus took one look at him and knew the man had sand; knew, in fact, seeing the look in the man's eyes, that he was going to draw on them.

Cyrus didn't wait for the man's hand to move. He plugged him in the string tie and dropped him.

Folks started screaming, so Cyrus fired another round into the ceiling.

"Next one of you who screams gets what he got," Cyrus informed them as the twins, Bo and Hardy Bannerman, spread out and put their scatterguns on the tellers. Slick and Wyatt stayed close to the door. "The bank manager has three seconds to get out here with his hands up."

It only took him two.

He looked about a hundred and ten years old, but apparently, he still had something to live for, because he hurried right out there and everything was, "Yes, sir. Whatever you say, sir," from the get-go.

The old man even ordered everybody in the bank to just do

as they were told and nobody would get hurt.

Which was not true, of course. But hey, let them think it, if it would speed things up.

Two minutes later, the vault was open and empty, and Cyrus and his crew were two thousand dollars richer.

As planned, Deekins corralled everyone into the vault so none of them could get squirrelly and backshoot the gang.

"You," Cyrus said, pointing at the younger woman. Up close, she wasn't much to look at, but she'd do. These townsfolk were sodbusters and shopkeepers. They saw a woman riding double with Cyrus, they'd never risk the shot. "You're coming with me."

She gasped when he grabbed her wrist but knew better than to resist, apparently remembering what happened to the man in the white shirt.

"Here comes the sheriff," Wyatt announced calmly from beside the door. He sounded almost amused. "He's got three men with him, two with rifles, one wearing an apron and packing a pistol."

The sheriff first, Cyrus thought. *Then the riflemen. Leave the shopkeeper for me.*

That very second, the Sharps boomed loudly from across the street—once, twice, three times—and just like that, three of the four men were down. First the sheriff, then the riflemen.

The startled shopkeeper dropped his pistol, which discharged, making the man jump as he lifted his hands in the air.

Cyrus pushed through the door, dragging the woman along with him, and shot the shopkeeper in the head.

The gang mounted up.

"Where are you taking me?" the woman demanded, finally finding her voice as Cyrus hauled her onto the saddle in front of him. "I am a married woman. I have a family."

"Don't worry, ma'am. It won't be but a short trip."

As they started riding, someone down the street opened fire with a rifle.

Bo Bannerman set to cussing when a round burned his arm, but then the Sharps boomed again, and the shooting down the street stopped.

They rode hard, heading west out of town, the men firing as they went, dropping a few fools who came running out to stop them.

Once they'd gotten safely outside of town, Cyrus stopped and let the woman down from his horse.

"Told you it'd be a short trip," Cyrus said.

She wobbled, looking faint, but sighed with relief. "Thank you, sir."

Then he shot her in the forehead and rode off.

CHAPTER 6

J ustice rode through the slashing rain, soaked to his skin despite his long slicker. It had been coming in sideways for the better part of an hour, and to his left, the Rio Grande thundered, its churning payload of stone and timber pounding the banks.

Beneath him, Dagger trudged on, surefooted as ever, the most magnificent stallion this side of Fredericksburg, Texas. Perhaps Dagger was even the superior of Bourbon.

Justice wasn't worried about splitting hairs on that question. He was just grateful to own two such magnificent animals.

He sometimes entertained the notion of bringing Bourbon to Dos Pesos, but no ranch in the world was big enough to house two such stallions. Sooner or later, they would battle for supremacy, and given their size and strength and endurance, they might just both die in the fight.

He wouldn't risk it. Instead, he left Bourbon in Texas,

knowing Matt and Luke both exercised the powerful stallion and gave him the best of treatment.

"Need to find us a place to hole up, boy," he said, smoothing a hand over Dagger's muscular neck. "Be dark soon."

It looked like he'd be going without a fire tonight. Which wouldn't be so bad if it didn't also mean going without coffee.

By his lights, any camp without coffee was an abomination.

But no sooner had these thoughts passed through his mind than he topped a rise and saw lights burning in the distance. Through the gathering gloom, he could make out a farmhouse and a small barn perched on a bench above the river. He saw the dark forms of several cows bunched miserably in the rain.

Even through the heavy rain, Justice noticed the ranch was falling into disrepair. The structures still looked solid enough, but vines were creeping up the barn, and beyond the small vegetable patch, the main field lay fallow beneath a tall stand of weeds.

And yet someone was undoubtedly home. Lights shone in the windows. Above the chimney, smoke swirled and broke apart in the rain and faded into the impending twilight.

"Hello, the house!" he called and waited there atop Dagger, not wanting to dismount unless someone invited him to do so.

The door swung halfway open, and a gun barrel slid into view.

Justice put a hand on one revolver but did not pull the weapon.

A dark-haired boy a couple of years older than Eli followed the barrel. His big eyes searched the rain-streaked gloom and finally found Justice.

The barrel came up a touch but did not swing toward Justice. "Who are you?" the boy called.

"Name's Justice. Was hoping you folks would let my horse and me spend the night in your barn. I'll pay for the hay and any grub or coffee you can spare. It's coming down something fierce out here."

From behind the boy, a woman's voice spoke, but between distance and the rain, Justice couldn't make out any words.

The boy asked, "Where are you coming from, mister?"

"Dos Pesos. I'm headed for Taos."

"You're not from around these parts?"

"I am not."

There was a brief pause filled with muffled voices. Then the boy lowered the barrel and spoke again. "Mama says you're more than welcome."

Justice touched the brim of his hat. "Much obliged. I'm gonna get old Dagger out of the rain. I'll settle up with you in the morning if that suits you and your mama."

The woman appeared beside the boy, half-silhouetted by the lights within. She stooped, leaning on a cane.

Not the boy's mother, then. His grandmother.

But then she shifted, stepping into the light, and he saw that she was no older than he, probably right around thirty.

"You see to your horse, Mister Justice," she said, "then come on back to the house. We'll keep the stew warm for you."

Justice touched the brim of his hat. "Much obliged, ma'am. My horse put in a day's work and deserves a good rubdown."

The woman nodded. "A good man tends to his horse before he tends to himself. Take your time, Mr. Justice, and we'll be glad for your company. You'll find a lantern hanging inside the door. There's grain and hay both. Help yourself, and if you run into any trouble, Miguel will come out and give you a hand."

"I appreciate that, ma'am, but I should be all right. You folks go ahead and enjoy your supper. I apologize for interrupting."

He rode through the pouring rain to the barn and got down and opened the door, and half a dozen skittish cats went scampering into the deeper recesses.

Inside, everything was dry and nice and smelled like heaven. Justice had always loved the smell of a horse barn, especially one like this with plenty of hay and mucked-out stalls.

Dagger's hooves clopped hollowly across the floorboards, and from the darkness, horses blew and nickered. One of them kicked the wall hard, but whether it was a challenge or just excitement, Justice could not say, not without seeing the animal.

Dagger stood tall and proud and silent, nostrils flared, ears erect, as Justice took down the lantern and lit it and removed the saddle and went to work, rubbing Dagger down with one of several towels hanging in the nearest stall, which was empty save for a stool, a few hand tools, and various bits of tack draped over its sides.

Once he'd finished drying and massaging the stallion's big muscles, he spoke softly as he ran a curry comb over him.

Then he led him into an empty stall and fetched a bucket of water and some grain. After Dagger had finished the grain, Justice forked hay into the stall.

Again, he was impressed by the cleanliness and order of the barn. Taken with the outer state of disrepair, it spoke of an overwhelmed family choosing how to spend its limited time.

Up and down the stable, horses continued to snort and

whinny, but there was no banging around and no more kicking. They watched Dagger with great interest, eyes rolling and glistening in the flickering illumination of the lantern.

Outside, dark had fallen. The wind had picked up and was driving the rain almost sideways.

Across the way, the small house hunched in the weather, dark save for two dimly lit windows.

There was trouble here.

He could feel that.

Now, it was time to go inside and find out exactly what that trouble was.

CHAPTER 7

Justice strode across the yard and knocked on the door, which swung open at once to reveal a family of three, all of them with jet-black hair.

The tall, gangly boy, Miguel, held the door. The mother leaned on her cane near the stove and offered a grimacing smile. At the table sat a very cute pigtailed girl two or three years younger than Eli.

The woman introduced herself as Alameda Sanchez. The girl they called Angelica.

"Very nice to meet you, Mrs. Sanchez," Justice said, sweeping his hat from his head. "Again, I'm much obliged."

Mrs. Sanchez told Justice to take off his wet slicker. She set to ladling him a bowl of stew while he hung up his wet coat, noting another man's jacket hanging from one of the pegs.

Where was Mr. Sanchez?

Mrs. Sanchez set his bowl at the head of the table, opposite of where she sat.

Justice bowed his head in silent prayer then had at it, savoring the rich beef stew and a heel of buttered bread.

"Ma'am, this food is wonderful. And that's not the wet ride talking. This is top-notch fare."

Mrs. Sanchez gave a slight nod of her head. Despite her relative youth, silver strands streaked her dark hair. "It does my heart good to see a man eat, Mr. Justice."

Miguel drooped at these words and stared into his own bowl, while little Angelica, clearly enamored with Justice, kept sneaking glances and grinning.

He set down his spoon and covered his face then swung open his hands in a game of peek-a-boo that utterly delighted the cheerful toddler.

Mrs. Sanchez watched, smiling sadly. "Her father likes to play that game with her, too. I wish he was feeling well enough to come out and meet you."

"I wish he was, too. You have a nice home here. I'm always happy to meet hardworking folks who make the world a better place. I believe most people are good. But it only takes a few bad ones to destroy whatever the good ones build."

"That is true, Mr. Justice," Mrs. Sanchez said, and laid her cane atop the table. "You strike me as a good man. And because you are a good man, I will share a warning: avoid the Crossroads Saloon three miles north of here."

"Rough place?"

She shook her head. "Not especially, no. But lately, someone has been lurking outside the saloon. They wait for men who have had too much to drink and—"

Miguel pounded his fist on the table. "The cowards hit Papa

from behind. Hit him and broke his skull and stole his money and his horse."

"I'm awful sorry to hear that," Justice said.

Now, even the little girl looked sad. In fact, Angelica's big eyes welled up with tears. "I miss Papa," she cried.

Miguel rose and scooped up Angelica and set to bouncing her, shushing her in a loving embrace.

"My son speaks the truth," Mrs. Sanchez said. "These robbers hit Enrico from behind and nearly killed him. In fact, it would have been a mercy if they had sent him to the Lord. He has not awakened for weeks."

"Don't give up hope, ma'am."

Mrs. Sanchez brightened. "Are you a doctor?"

"No, ma'am, but something similar happened to me once, and I didn't wake up for a month. I was weak as a kitten when I came to, and I couldn't remember hardly anything, but with the help of my wife and son and a few good friends, I came around again."

Encouraged, they led Justice to the back of the house, where an emaciated Mr. Sanchez lay pale and corpselike in a small, foul-smelling room.

"Is there anything we can do for him?" Mrs. Sanchez asked. "Do you have any suggestions, Mr. Justice?"

Staring down at the dying man, Justice's heart broke for these poor people. "Pray."

"We pray morning, noon, and night, Mr. Justice."

"Spend time with him. Talk to him. He might hear more than you think. I hope he's back on his feet soon."

He said it, and he meant it—he did hope the man was back on his feet soon—but he sure didn't expect the wish to come true. Sanchez was too far gone. Must be tough to hang on this long. Must be holding on for something.

They led Justice back out into the kitchen, and while Mrs. Sanchez boiled a pot of coffee, Miguel fetched a guitar and played in a soulful Spanish style that touched Justice's heart and set his star-shaped scar to burning.

When the boy finished, Justice complimented him, sipped the hot, dark coffee, and said, "Tell me more about this saloon."

CHAPTER 8

"Get you another, young fella?" the white-haired bartender asked.

Justice slumped at the bar. He looked up slowly, blinked at the bartender, and nodded drunkenly. "Hit me again, bar dog."

Leaning against the worn plank, Justice wobbled, pretending to be oblivious of the boisterous crowd around him.

The Crossroads Saloon stood at the ragged edge of a ratty town called Sledge. The only saloon for miles around, the Crossroads was dirty and dim and smelled of spilled beer and the stink of the men packing it.

The bartender tipped a bottle and filled Justice's glass with rotgut.

Justice pulled a fistful of money from his slicker pocket and made a show of trying to sort out what he owed, squinting at the greenbacks and golden coins.

"This'll do, sonny," the bartender said, quickly palming a golden eagle.

Justice nodded sleepily and pawed at the money, stuffing it awkwardly into his pocket again, letting a greenback fall to the floor.

Out of the corner of his eye, he saw the bartender gesture to someone across the room.

Watching the bartender nod in his direction, Justice again lowered his whiskey glass between his legs and surreptitiously dumped its contents on the warped and sodden planking at his feet.

A moment later, a smiling young man cut through the crowd and bellied up to the bar beside Justice. Beneath a wide-brimmed, floppy hat and mop of light brown curls, the man's pale blue eyes looked amused as he clapped Justice on the shoulder. "Welcome to Sledge, partner. Let me buy you a drink. Hey, Finn, give me a beer and give my friend here whatever he's having."

"Coming right up, Curly," the bartender said with a sly smile.

"Obliged," Justice slurred and took a second to blink at Curly. "Last one. Drunk as a skunk."

Curly patted his shoulder again, really chumming it up. "That's why we come into saloons, partner. Enjoy. Here comes your whiskey now."

The bartender set the drinks in front of them. Justice noticed Curly paid nothing.

That's because the bartender expects to get his cut later, Justice thought. *He helped Curly rob all these people.*

Curly hoisted his beer in the air. "Come on, buddy. Bottoms up. Here's to your health."

"And good fortune," the bright-eyed bartender put in,

smiling at Curly.

"Drink… to… that," Justice slurred and swung his arm awkwardly, pretending to reach for the drink, and knocked it over instead. Amber liquid spilled across the bar.

Curly jerked his arm out of the way, and for a quarter of a second, his mask dropped away, revealing a snarling face flush with violence and contempt.

Curly quickly recovered, however. Smiling again, he took a sip from his beer and patted Justice on the back once more—a little harder this time, Justice noted.

"Looks like your cistern's full, partner," Curly said. "I've been there many a time. Tell you what, my friend. I'm gonna give you a hand. Me and this other friend of mine, Pepper—he's a good old boy—we'll walk you out. You show us your horse, and we'll help you mount up and get on your way."

Determined to play the part to the end, Justice waved him off. "Don't need no help."

Curly threw an arm around his shoulders. "Don't be like that, brother. I'm sure you'd give me a hand if the tables were turned, wouldn't you?"

Justice nodded, letting his eyelids laze most of the way shut.

"Where you staying tonight?"

Justice shrugged and grunted.

"No problem. I got just the place for you."

"Yeah," the bartender laughed. "You'll sleep like the dead."

Justice shrugged again.

It was all the permission Curly needed. He slipped his arm down Justice's back and helped him to his feet and led him toward the door.

Justice stumbled along as if in a drunken stupor.

Near the door, Curly called to a man named Pepper, and a tall, rawboned, broad-shouldered man in filthy buckskins stepped away from the wall. His small, sunken, piglike eyes burned with malice.

Pepper followed Curly and Justice into the foggy night. The door closed behind them, muffling the loud conversations of the drinkers in the saloon.

The night was damp. The air was much cooler than it had been inside.

Their boots crunched over the gravel outside.

"You're a biggun', friend," Curly laughed. "I'd hate to tangle with you when you're sober. Now which of these horses is yours?"

Justice grunted as if he didn't understand.

Curly repeated the question.

Justice nodded toward the end of the hitching rail, where Dagger stood as patient and magnificent as a statue.

"That there stallion?" Curly marveled. "Pepper, you ever see a finer horse?"

"He'll do," a surly voice said from only a few feet back. "Step aside, Curly."

Curly stepped to the side and held Justice's arm with one hand.

Hearing Pepper rush forward, Justice leaned forward and lashed out with a powerful mule kick. His boot heel sunk into Pepper's midsection.

Pepper grunted, left his feet, and flew off into the foggy darkness.

"Hey!" a startled Curly shouted and made the mistake of trying to restrain Justice.

Justice's palm strike caught him under the chin and sat him down hard on the gravel.

Not wanting to fight two men at once, Justice kicked the fallen Curly in the side of the head and knocked him out, then turned just in time to see Pepper rushing out of the fog, arm raised, swinging the black sap he had undoubtedly used to crush the skulls of numerous victims.

But the mugger's luck had run out.

Justice blocked his wrist and blasted him with a right hand. The punch landed square. He felt Pepper's nose shatter beneath his knuckles and felt that telling jolt you feel when you catch somebody clean, and they go loose in their boots.

Pepper dropped to the gravel with a crunch, convulsed, and went still.

Justice considered gut shooting the men like they deserved. But he didn't want to make the noise. If folks came rushing out and got the wrong idea, he might end up having to hurt or kill innocent people.

Besides, he still had business with the bartender who'd set him up.

Moving quickly, he gagged the unconscious men and pulled pigging strips from his pocket.

Seconds later, he had their wrists tied behind their backs and had hobbled their ankles so they would be able to shuffle at best.

When they came to again, he held his pistol on them.

Both men struggled briefly then stared up at him.

"You boys probably already figured this out, but I wasn't really drunk, not like those other folks you followed outside.

Now, I've got some questions, and you're gonna answer every last one of them."

CHAPTER 9

Finn closed early. Greed, which lived always inside him like a dark beast curled around his heart, protested mightily, since he had a pretty good crowd, but common sense prevailed.

Something had happened to Curly and Pepper.

Which didn't seem possible.

The tall man had sat there for hours, drinking straight whiskey, and never would've even made the door if Curly hadn't helped him.

Finn thought again of the man's greenbacks and golden coins and reckoned he knew exactly what had happened.

Curly and Pepper had finally struck it big. After the dozens of drunks Finn had fed them, they had finally rolled somebody packing hundreds or maybe even thousands of dollars.

They'd done in the tall man, found the loot, and taken off with Finn's share of the money, a full third. It was his bar, after all, and he was the one who had softened wayward travelers and set Curly on their tracks.

Finn shook his head as he pulled the sawed-off shotgun from beneath the bar. He'd always known that sooner or later Curly and Pepper would pull something like this.

Well, he'd show them. Nobody cheated Dawson Finn and lived to tell the tale. Why, he'd been fighting tougher men than them for decades before they'd even been born.

Yes, he'd show Curly and Pepper, all right.

Then, after things died down, he'd recruit two other men to do his strong-arm work. Thieves and killers were a dime a dozen out here on the frontier.

But first, he had a score to settle.

Without even bothering to sweep up the broken glass, Finn snuffed all the lamps except one lantern, which he took outside.

Holding the stubby scattergun at his beltline, Finn swept the lantern back and forth, squinting into the night. He doubted Curly and Pepper had the guts to go up against him, but you couldn't be too careful.

Unfortunately, the light barely penetrated the fog, which continued to drift off the swollen river, swirling like an army of writhing ghosts.

And suddenly, he was sick of this place, sick of this life, sick to death of it. He was gonna catch these no-good thieves, take the money, add it to the thousand dollars he had at the house, and cash in his chips. Burn this stinking saloon to the ground and head for the West Coast. Get a boat, do some fishing, and, if he needed more money, well, he had a knack for spotting suckers. He'd just set up another operation in California.

Yes, California.

He walked the muddy path to his house, which stood dark as a tomb a hundred yards back at the edge of the woods.

But as he drew close to the house, Finn got a funny feeling, the icy fingers of dread tickling up his spine.

Curly and Pepper knew he had money. If this was indeed their big break, would they be satisfied with whatever they took off the tall man?

No. Not even if it was ten thousand dollars.

Men like them were never satisfied.

But did they have the guts to lie in wait for Finn?

It didn't seem likely, but you never knew. Greed was a powerful magnifier of bravery when men like these two scoundrels smelled gold.

He extinguished his lantern, set it on the ground, and crept forward with the shotgun, following the path by memory and the feel of his feet.

With the lantern extinguished, his eyes adapted, and as he drew closer, he saw a faint and flickering light coming from behind his house.

What if Curley and Pepper were rooting through his place right now?

Picturing the filthy pigs prying up his floorboards, he shouldered the shotgun and rushed forward, ready to kill.

But when he came around the corner of the house and saw the scene behind his home, he realized just how wrong he'd been.

Curly and Pepper were not robbing him. In fact, it was safe to say they would never rob anyone again. They hung from the upper limbs of the cottonwood, their eyes bulging eerily in death.

Finn's chairs and what looked like the last remnants of his bedding burned in a heap, illuminating the ghastly scene and the freshly painted sign pounded into the ground between the flickering fire and the bodies swaying in the wind.

These three men conspired to kill drunks leaving the Crossroads Saloon, the sign announced. *Justice has been served.*

Finn reread the sign. *Three men?* he wondered. *There's only two.*

Then, he lifted his eyes and with a jolt of terror spotted the third noose hanging empty between his dead partners in crime.

Cursing, Finn stumbled backward, still staring with horror at the scene, and reached for the back door.

But his hand met only empty air.

Meaning the door had been opened.

Meaning—

An iron grip seized Finn and yanked him into the door jam, knocking his shotgun to the ground.

He barely had time to scream before that iron grip hauled him into the darkness.

CHAPTER 10

"Did you bring your buggy this afternoon, or would you like to have these items shipped, Mrs. Bullard?" the smiling Mr. Mueller said from behind the counter of Mueller's Mercantile.

"We brought the buggy today, thank you," Nora said.

"Very well, ma'am. If you would like to pull the buggy up front, I'll have the stove and heavy sacks loaded for you."

"Thank you, Mr. Mueller."

"My pleasure, Mrs. Bullard, and thank you for your business. Now, will that be all, or shall I wait for the children?"

"Yes, please do wait for the children. I'll let each of them get a little something."

Eli studied the hard candy, grinning. He'd lost another tooth. Nora found his patchy smile rather endearing.

Katie was farther back in the store, studying not candy but Mr. Mueller's rack of books. She had one open to the middle, and her eyes flicked back and forth, reading.

"If I am not mistaken," Mr. Mueller said, furrowing his brow with confusion, "Katie already owns all of those books."

"Likely so," Nora laughed. "She's probably just rereading one of them… again. Some of those books, she's probably read ten times."

Mr. Mueller, a reader himself, nodded with approval. "Excellent."

Seeing no reason to hurry the children, Nora drifted toward the fabric. She lingered over a new roll of light blue material, testing its quality with her thumb and forefinger.

It felt quite nice, and the price wasn't bad.

Thanks to Justice, she could now afford to purchase clothing for herself and her family, but no matter how much money they had in their bank account, thrift remained a virtue, and Nora continued to make their clothing herself.

She was just imagining how pretty Katie would look in a dress of the light blue fabric when a voice behind her spoke softly.

"Excuse me, Mrs. Bullard?"

"Yes?" Nora said, turning to face a young man she'd never seen before. Tall and lean with a boyish face and wavy, long blond hair, he wore new-looking jeans, a clean white shirt, and a nervous expression. He clutched his hat at his beltline in hands that looked too large even for the rest of him.

"Ma'am," the boy said, "my name's Lonnie Cooper, ma'am, and I was wondering if… What I mean to say, ma'am, is folks were saying you might possibly have work on your ranch?"

"Nice to meet you, Lonnie, and yes, we always have plenty of work on our ranch. What sort of work are you hoping to find?"

The boy straightened, his nervousness vanishing with her question. "I'm a cowboy, ma'am. I can rope, ride, brand 'em, and break 'em. Whatever you need done, I'll see to it. When I sign on, I ride for the brand."

Nora smiled, liking this sincere if awkward young man. "You have experience?"

"Oh yes, ma'am. I've driven cattle to Denver, Cheyenne, Omaha, all over. I'm first out and last in, ma'am. I go from can to can't day after day. Here, ma'am. This here's my bona fides."

Lonnie pulled a folded sheet of paper from his shirt pocket and fumbled awkwardly to unfold, straighten, and extend the letter in her direction.

Nora took it and read the single sentence scrawled in a crude but legible script.

This here letter sertifys that Lonnie Cooper is a top hand.

Under this, someone had marked a large X in grease pencil.

"That there is trail boss Elroy Pavey's mark. You can tell by that little barb he makes off the top of the X. See there?"

"Did you do the writing?"

Suddenly, the boy looked a bit sheepish again. "No, ma'am. I ain't had no book learning to speak of. Mr. Pavey spoke the words just like that, called me a top hand, and my friend Denny Hollenback wrote it up, and Mr. Pavey set his mark to it."

"Well," Nora said, folding the paper and handing it back to the boy, "thank you for sharing that with me, Lonnie. Do you have a horse?"

"Oh yes, ma'am. I got me the best da—" For a second, Lonnie looked like he'd swallowed a fly. "What I mean to say, ma'am, is I got me the best darn mustang you ever done saw. Broke him myself. He's a desert horse. Smart as a collie and climbs mountains like a goat." He chuckled. "You should see him come down the other side, ma'am. He squats right down and slides on his backside."

Nora couldn't help but smile.

"But to answer your question, ma'am, yes, I got me a top-notch cattle horse and all the gear I need. A good saddle, rope, a Winchester, and my Colt. All I need is a brand to ride for."

Saying this, he slapped the revolver on his hip.

"Do you know how to use it?"

"Yes, ma'am."

"And the rifle?"

"Yes, ma'am. I can shoot. You folks having trouble?"

"Not at the moment, but we've had more than our share in the past, so we've learned to hire men who can fight."

"I never run from a fight all my life, ma'am."

"I'm glad to hear that, Lonnie. When could you start?"

Lonnie smiled. "Anytime, ma'am. The sooner the better. I don't work cattle for a few days, I get downright twitchy."

"Well, we can't have that. My husband's out of town for the moment, but why don't you come back to the ranch with us? I'll introduce you to the other hands and hire you on a trial period until my husband returns. You do a good job, and I'm confident he'll hire you on permanently."

"Thank you for the opportunity, ma'am."

"My pleasure, Lonnie. A dollar a day and found?"

Smiling he stuck out his big hand. "It's a deal, ma'am."

Nora chuckled at the boy's earnest enthusiasm and shook his hand. Despite his youthful nature, his hands were rough with callouses, and though he was gentle with her, she could feel the strength coursing through that grip.

Justice will like him, she thought, and Eli appeared at her side and waved at Lonnie. "Hello, sir."

Lonnie crouched down and stuck out his hand again. "Hello, partner. My name's Lonnie."

Eli shook the big hand and looked Lonnie in the eyes with a solemn expression on his face, mirroring his pa, Justice. "Good to meet you, Lonnie."

"Lonnie, I'll settle up with Mr. Mueller, and then would you please give me a hand loading the buggy?"

"Yes, ma'am."

"Katie, come along, dear," she called to the copper-haired girl, who jumped a little, startled out of her reading.

"Sorry, Mama," Katie said, replacing the book and coming forward. "I had just gotten to the part where—"

Spotting Lonnie, Katie stopped in her tracks and lost her voice.

At the same moment, Lonnie's eyes bulged, spotting Katie, and he blushed, pinkening his tanned face.

Nora's eyes shifted to her daughter, whose face had turned so red her freckles had vanished.

"Lonnie, this is my daughter, Katie. Katie, this is Lonnie. He's going to be working on our ranch."

Lonnie dipped his head. "Nice to meet you, Miss Katie."

"It's my pleasure, sir," Katie said in a soft voice and gave a little curtsy.

Inwardly, Nora was amused by the awkwardness of the two teenagers. It was the first time she'd ever seen Katie show interest in a boy.

But what kind of boy was Lonnie Cooper? From what she understood, cowboys were romantics at heart, but she'd heard men could be rather crude on the trail, too.

She'd just have to keep her eye on them until Justice came home.

Which raised another question: how would Justice handle a young man showing interest in his little girl?

CHAPTER 11

Justice took care of Dagger and stabled him for the night and crossed the yard toward the Sanchez house.

Dim light flickered weakly in the kitchen. They had left a light on for him.

It was late. What time, exactly, he did not know. Likely on the darker side of midnight, anyhow.

The rain had stopped. Strong winds out of the south carried off the fog and parted the clouds overhead, creating a river of stars that twinkled across the dome of night.

He opened the door silently, not wanting to wake the family.

"Were you successful?" Mrs. Sanchez's voice asked from the deeper shadows beyond the light of the flickering candle upon the dinner table.

"I was, ma'am."

Mrs. Sanchez stepped into view, leaning on her cane at the edge of candlelight, her features drawn and hard. "And the men?"

"Dead, ma'am. They're all dead."

Mrs. Sanchez closed her eyes and just stood there for a few silent seconds.

When she opened them again, she wore the slightest of smiles. "Thank you, Mr. Justice. Tonight, for the first time in weeks, I will sleep well."

Justice touched the brim of his hat. "Happy to help, ma'am. They had it coming to them. Here."

He reached inside his slicker, pulled out the heavy sack of money he'd discovered in Dawson Finn's home, and dropped it on the table with a loud clinking of golden coins.

Mrs. Sanchez raised a hand to her mouth. "What's that?"

"It's money, ma'am."

"But where—"

"The saloonkeeper had it. He was the ringleader."

Mrs. Sanchez reached out timidly and poked the sack. "How much money is this?"

"A good deal, ma'am. I'd say a thousand dollars, maybe more."

"A thousand…" Her voice trailed off as she stared at the sack with apparent awe.

"I hope it helps you."

"Me?"

"Yes, ma'am. It's yours now."

"But Enrico only had a few dollars."

Justice spread his hands. "This work I do, it's not precise, ma'am. I do what I can. Unfortunately, I don't have time to track down all the folks who might lay claim to some of this money. I gotta move on and see to other troubles. But giving this money to you sets things right in my mind."

"Are you a lawman?"

He shook his head. "I set things right."

She looked at him, obviously curious, but pressed no further. "Well, I thank you for your generosity, Mr. Justice. Perhaps if I ask around, I will be able to determine others who deserve a share."

"With all due respect, ma'am, I wouldn't mention this money to anyone."

Her mouth opened a little. "Do you think there might be trouble with the law?"

"Perhaps. I reckon there's a better chance, though, of trouble on the other side of that coin."

"You think these men had friends?"

He shook his head. "I reckon I burned the hornet's nest. But sadly, some folks hear about a pile of money, and it brings out the worst in them."

Mrs. Sanchez stared into the darkness, the flickering light rippling across her dark pupils.

Then she nodded. "I understand, Mr. Justice."

"I'm glad to hear that, ma'am."

"I am very tired. I think, perhaps, it's because I finally know things have been set right."

Justice nodded.

"Is there anything I can get for you, Mr. Justice, before I retire? Stew? Coffee?"

"No, ma'am. I'm much obliged to have a dry spot to spread my bedroll. In the morning, ma'am, I'd like to take Miguel hunting if that's all right with you."

"Yes, of course. But Miguel is not a hunter."

"He'll need to become one to keep meat on the table. I'll

show him a few things. We'll set out before first light. Before breakfast, I mean. It's good to hunt on an empty stomach. Gives you an edge. I'll teach Miguel what I can."

"Thank you."

"I can give you meat or money, but sooner or later, you'll run out. It's not enough to help folks. I try to help folks help themselves."

Mrs. Sanchez stared at him for a moment. "Are you real?"

"Ma'am?"

"I'm sorry, it's just… I'm very tired. Goodnight, Mr. Justice."

"Goodnight, ma'am."

CHAPTER 12

"Drizzly morning like this," Justice whispered, "deer'll lay low."

Miguel, carrying Justice's Winchester, nodded.

Justice's eyes swept from side to side until they locked onto the dark green stand of conifers girding the base of the hillside at the opposite end of the field.

"They're likely holed up in them pines," he told the boy. "Probably bedded down in the rain and haven't bothered to get up yet. Pick up your feet when you walk, son. If you scuff, deer will hear you coming."

"Yes, sir."

Justice put the boy on watch at the edge of the field. Speaking in light whispers, he questioned Miguel again about the rifle and where to aim.

"And you make good and sure of your target before you pull the trigger."

"Yes, sir."

"I reckon the deer will come out of those trees. You stand real still and don't make a noise. I'll be back."

Justice turned and walked along the edge of the field, then moved silently into a stand of aspens. Taking his time, he walked parallel to the hillside, then followed a narrow creek uphill.

It was easy to move silently across the sodden ground, and he knew any sound he made would be muffled by the stream. The air was still and damp. Runoff pattered in all directions. Topping a ridge, he moved slowly down the slope. The aspens gave way to a gloomy stand of white pines.

Halfway down the hill, he heard a deer's sharp snort. With pounding hooves and snapping branches, several deer leapt up from their beds and pounded downhill away from him. Their white tails bobbed up and down as they charged out of the pines and into the field.

Come on, kid, he thought.

A shot rang out, and Justice heard the tell-tale thump of a bullet hitting meat broadside.

He kept walking down the hill. There was no more shooting, which meant the kid either missed or made a clean kill.

As Justice came off the hill, the sun broke over the horizon and illuminated the field.

Miguel stood there smiling with the rifle over one shoulder.

Justice walked over and looked down at the dead eight-point lying at the boy's feet.

"I got him," Miguel said.

"I see that." Justice's eyes found the small hole behind the deer's shoulder. "Good shooting."

"Thank you, sir."

"You got your knife?"

"Yes, sir."

"You ever gut a deer before?"

"No, sir."

"All right, son. I'm gonna teach you."

Lifting one of the buck's legs, Justice showed the boy where to start, explaining how to make each cut and why each mattered.

As the boy worked, Justice said, "You want good tasting venison, harvest a young doe. But if your herd is small, take a buck. Doe'll have two babies next spring, build the herd. Now, you want to be careful with this next cut. Use just the tip of the knife. Get it under the skin there and no deeper. You nick the stomach, it'll be the worst thing you ever smelled."

The boy worked with great focus, doing as he was told.

Which was good. Because Miguel would have to be the man of the family now. He had to learn this here and now, because the most basic thing a man must do is put meat on the table.

After they removed the entrails, Justice said, "Be real careful after you cut the diaphragm and reach up inside. Could be a jagged rib just waiting to slice you."

The boy proceeded with caution and managed to finish the job without hurting himself.

"Tuck the heart and liver back inside and come on," Justice said, starting back across the field.

"We're just gonna leave him here, sir?"

"Only for a moment, son. We're gonna go back and get your horse. I'll teach you how to hitch a drag rope. You shot a big ol' buck, and there's no sense wearing ourselves out, dragging him home, not when we have a horse to do the work for us. That's another thing, son. Stay busy, do your work, but always conserve your energy, because you never know what might be coming around the bend."

The boy listened with reverence.

He was a good kid, and Justice hated to leave him and his family, but he knew he had to.

When he'd lost his memory, he'd gotten tangled up with some bad folks, and he'd kept on fighting until they were dead, and he had most of the answers he needed to sort out his life.

But now, back on the trail again, he was remembering what it meant, roaming the world as a silent justice.

It meant stopping bad men. It meant helping folks when you could. It meant setting things right.

But you had to keep moving. There were too many bad men and too many good people who needed too much help.

You could never really set things right.

Because that wasn't the way of the world.

It's easier to destroy than rebuild. And with so many folks tearing things down, he had to come to terms with his limitations.

He could only do so much. Then folks had to do for themselves.

They went into the stable and got Miguel's horse and a rope and went back out to the deer, and Justice taught the boy the best way to set up the drag, and Miguel thanked him and said, "My daddy's going to die, isn't he?"

Justice looked down at the boy. In the early morning light, Miguel's face looked young and pale and frightened.

"I reckon so, son."

The boy nodded and turned away.

Justice remained silent, giving the kid a moment, and busied himself with the saddle while Miguel's shoulders hitched up and down, the boy doing his best to muffle the sound of his sobbing.

When Miguel finally wiped away his tears and settled his breathing, Justice spoke without turning. "It's a hard world."

"Yes, sir. You killed them, though."

"I did."

"Doesn't really change anything, though."

Now, Justice looked at him. "No?"

Miguel shook his head. "Killing them doesn't bring Papa back."

"No, it doesn't. But killing those men was justice, and I believe justice matters."

Miguel was silent for a moment. "Yes, sir. I shouldn't have said anything. I wasn't thinking."

"You were thinking, son. And I understand. I wish I could make things better. I wish I could heal good people or bring folks back from the dead, but God did not see fit to give me those powers. All I can do is make sure that people like the men who hurt your daddy don't go hurting anybody else."

"I'm glad they're dead, sir."

"Every man must do what he thinks is right, son. It'll never be enough, but it's what we've got, so we do it. Do you understand?"

"Yes, sir. I'll try to do like you said. I'll try to do what's right, to make things better."

"I know you will, son," Justice said, patting Miguel on the back. "I know you will."

————

THE REST OF THAT DAY, JUSTICE HELPED THE SANCHEZES AS BEST he could.

That night, he woke abruptly and blinked up into the darkness.

Outside, the rain had started up again.

He listened to it beat against the roof and gurgle in the eaves and knew, somehow, that Mr. Sanchez had died.

He did not know how he knew and didn't waste time wondering.

After that, he merely dozed, waiting for the others to wake.

He did not want to stay. He did not want to witness their pain, did not want to hear Mrs. Sanchez explain everything to little Angelica.

But he would stay. Because it was the right thing to do.

He would wait for them and help them. Then he would leave. It was time to get back on the trail. It was time to track down Jasper Falco and keep him from killing again.

And then he would return to his own family and hold each of his loved ones just a little tighter.

CHAPTER 13

The next day, as Justice helped Miguel dig a grave in the muddy ground beyond the house, Nora sat in her own home, mending one of Eli's torn shirts, when the boy himself came running in, huffing and puffing, eyes wide with obvious excitement.

"Mama, come quick! Mr. Lonnie is fixing to break that new mustang!"

"Thank you, Eli. I will be out."

The boy was gone in a flash. How Nora loved her son, his pleading voice, his gushing enthusiasm, his fascination over all things masculine—well, except, perhaps, for his fascination with poker.

"How exciting," Katie said. "May I watch, too, Mama?"

Nora set down her mending and got to her feet. "Come along, dear. I suppose now we'll see whether or not our new employee exaggerated his qualifications. That new paint is just about the craziest mustang I've ever seen."

They went outside and walked to the corral and joined Eli, Clem, and the other men at the rail.

The mustang stood on the far side of the corral, blowing loudly and staring at Lonnie, who nodded in their direction before starting forward on his own stallion.

"How come he doesn't have the mustang side hobbled?" Eli asked. "There's no sack or nothing."

How come, indeed, Nora thought, figuring Lonnie meant to show off a little.

The wild-eyed mustang started to the right, then broke quickly to the left, sticking to the rail as Lonnie, moving effortlessly atop his mahogany bay, spun the lariat overhead.

The bay cut an angle, the mustang bunched up, and Lonnie had the rope over its neck.

"Oh," Katie gasped. Her eyes stared feverishly at the young cowboy. "Did you see that, Mama? He got him the first try."

Repressing a smile, Nora said, "Yes, he did."

Lonnie hauled on the rope and locked it tight.

For a time, the mustang struggled. But Lonnie choked him into exhaustion, and the wild stallion went to the ground close to where they stood.

Lonnie dismounted with a hackamore and went over to the mustang and got down with him and lowered his face to the nose of the semi-conscious stallion.

"What's he doing, Mama?" Eli asked. "Is he smooching the horse?"

Nora said nothing and watched the boy's cheeks billow and flatten as he breathed air into the mustang's nostrils.

"Old Indian trick," a clearly impressed Clem commented.

Lonnie whispered softly to the mustang as he slipped the

hackamore over its head, his every motion strong and natural and confident.

A short time later, he let the horse up and stood holding a long rope attached to the hackamore.

"That was amazing," Katie said breathlessly.

Lonnie gave her a quick smile then turned to Nora. "Ma'am, if you'll have one of these men bring me your gentlest mare, we'll tie 'em together. I'll work with him and make him follow her for a few days. Then I'll take him down to the river and break him in the deep water. I reckon he'll be a real nice riding horse in no time, ma'am."

"Very well, Lonnie," Nora said. "I look forward to seeing the finished product."

"Yes, ma'am. Proof's in the pudding."

"I've never seen anything like that, Lonnie," Katie gushed. "Never, ever, ever."

He tipped his hat. "Well, thank you for saying that, Miss Katie. You're very kind."

Nora took the girl's arm and turned to go.

Well, she thought, feeling her daughter tremble against her, *I now know two things: Lonnie did not exaggerate his qualifications, and I am definitely going to have to watch Katie around him.*

CHAPTER 14

J ustice bounced the reluctant bartender's face off the bar just hard enough to make him understand the situation.

The man stepped back, clutching his nose. His watering eyes, which had been so sullen and self-assured seconds earlier, now gleamed with fear.

"Does that jog your memory?" Justice said.

"Hey," a big drunk in a dirty shirt said, coming to his feet starting across the mostly empty bar, "you leave Billy alone."

Justice shifted his gaze to the drunk.

The drunk hesitated, withered beneath Justice's stare, and returned to his seat and his beer.

Justice turned back to the bartender. "I've been following Falco for a long time. Trailed him to Taos then all the way here to Denver. Two different people told me that Falco came in here today. Now, are you gonna tell me the truth or force me to make you wish you had?"

The bartender shook his head, still clutching his broken

nose. "Okay, yeah, Falco was in here, all right? You missed him by half an hour."

"Tell me everything you know."

"He came in here, strutting like a game chicken, told me to give him a bottle of whiskey. I asked did he mean the whole bottle? And he got mad and put a hand on his six-shooter and said, 'What did I say? You need me to clean your ears out for you?'

"So I handed him the bottle and told him it was on the house. He nodded at that and got down to drinking. The more he drank, the more he talked."

"What did he tell you?"

"Said if I only knew who he was, I'd be shaking in my boots. Said he was a big man, an outlaw. Said he'd killed a sheriff."

"A deputy sheriff," Justice clarified. "But yeah, he's a killer. What else did he say?"

"Said everybody was going to know his name from coast-to-coast. He drank half the bottle then got up and said he was going to go to Nellie's and get his ashes hauled."

"Where's Nellie's?"

The bartender hooked a thumb to the right. "Next block over. You can't miss it. Girls stand out on the balcony in their underclothes and invite men up there."

"Much obliged," Justice said, and left the saloon.

When you got right down to it, Justice thought as he made his way down Blake Street, most killers were fools. They made it easy to find them.

Half of them were like Falco, so desperate to strut and brag that they were easier to find than a lost calf blatting for its mother.

They rarely covered their tracks and engendered no loyalty in others.

Like this bartender. He'd been afraid to tell Justice about Falco, but as soon as he realized that Justice was the more dangerous man, he'd rolled over like a puppy.

Well, like a normal puppy, anyway, he thought, wondering what Rafer's pups would be like. If they were anything like their father, they probably wouldn't go showing their belly without a fight.

He'd pick them up on the way home and see about that.

Reaching Nellie's, Justice ignored the women calling down to him from a third-floor balcony and went inside.

A well-dressed, middle-aged woman approached with a warm smile. "Good afternoon, sir. My name is Nellie, and my oh my, you certainly are a tall, good-looking gentleman. Looking for a little companionship?"

"Thank you, ma'am, but no." He held up his left hand and tapped the wedding ring.

"Congratulations, handsome. But I'm afraid if you're a happily married man that you have wandered into the wrong establishment. Nobody really comes in here for the tea and crackers."

"I don't imagine so," Justice chuckled. "Actually, ma'am, I'm on the trail of a dangerous man. He's killed two people I know of, and I believe he's getting a taste for it."

"Are you a lawman?"

"Something like that."

"A bounty hunter?"

"That's closer to the truth."

"What's this man's name?"

"Jasper Falco."

"I'm sorry, sir. I don't recognize his name."

"I believe he was here recently." Justice pulled the wanted poster from his pocket and held it up for Nellie.

Nellie's eyes brightened, and she nodded. "Yes, he came in here today. In fact, I believe he's still upstairs with Sylvie."

"Which room?"

"215. Second floor, third door on the left. Are you going to apprehend him?"

"Something like that."

"Don't hurt Sylvie. She's a nice girl."

"I will do everything I can to keep her safe, ma'am. Thank you." Justice put away the wanted poster and handed Nellie a $20 double eagle.

Nellie smiled and accepted the golden coin with a bat of her long lashes. "Why thank you, sir. That is very generous."

"Do me a favor and don't let anybody come up those stairs behind me, all right?" He didn't expect Falco to have any friends, but not expecting trouble was a good way to get yourself killed. "This shouldn't take but a minute."

Nellie agreed, and Justice pulled a Colt and started up the stairs.

He reached the second floor and listened hard. Somewhere down the hall beyond 215, bed springs squeaked, and a young woman moaned like she had a toothache.

He went to Sylvie's room and pressed an ear to the door and heard a man's voice say, "You want to come with me, darling? Hitch your wagon to a famous outlaw? Live a life of adventure?"

"No thank you, sir," a woman's voice said, sounding frightened. "I got my little daughter to think of."

"What if I decide to take you anyway?"

Justice had heard enough. Moving with exquisite slowness, he tried to turn the knob and found it locked.

"You could be my sidekick," Falco said. "You ever shoot a gun?"

Before Sylvie could respond, Justice drew back a boot and kicked the door as hard as he could. With a loud crack, the door swung open.

Sitting on the bed in a silk robe, Sylvie screamed.

Wearing only dungarees, Falco dove for the holster hanging on the bedpost.

"Don't even try it, Falco," Justice said. "I'm taking you in."

But the fugitive was dumbly committed to a course of action. He latched onto a pistol and yanked it free, shouting, "I'm a bad man!"

Calmly, Justice stepped to his right, taking Sylvie out of the line of fire.

Falco brought his weapon most of the way around, and Justice shot him in the eye patch.

Killed instantly, the self-proclaimed badman spilled backward and tumbled straight out the window.

Sylvie fainted.

The girls on the balcony upstairs set to screaming.

Justice walked over to the window, leaned out, and saw Falco lying dead on the ground.

"Well," he said to the unconscious woman as he reloaded his pistol, "that saves me having to carry him down the stairs."

CHAPTER 15

K atie sat on the porch of the newly finished guesthouse, helping Eli with his reading. He had made incredible progress since she'd joined the family several months earlier, and normally every word he read aloud was a pure joy to her.

Today, however, she was having a difficult time focusing because she had other things on her mind.

"How was that?" Eli asked, holding his place in the McGuffey reader with a freshly scrubbed finger.

Normally, Eli, like most boys, seemed to enjoy getting and staying dirty.

But when reading time came around, no one had to tell him to wash up. He would run inside and scrub his hands, not wanting to risk smudging the pages of his precious book.

Normally, his reverence amused and delighted Katie, but again, she had other things on her mind today.

Katie smiled, feeling a little guilty for her distraction. "Good job, Eli. I can't believe how well you're reading. Some of those words were hard."

"I like reading," Eli said. "Maybe someday, I'll read books like you do."

"I'm sure you will. And when you're ready, I'll lend you anything you wish to read."

Eli beamed, filling her heart with love. He was truly a brother to her now, and that made her so—

There, coming around the barn…

"Okay, Eli. Nice job. You run along now."

The boy was disappointed. "That's all we're gonna do? We hardly started, Katie."

"You go ahead, and I'll read more with you later. I have to speak with Mr. Lonnie for a moment."

Spotting Lonnie, Eli's eyes swelled. "I like Mr. Lonnie."

Katie smiled. "So do I. Very much, in fact. Run along now, Eli."

"Okay. Bye!"

Eli scampered toward the main house, waving enthusiastically, and called out as he passed Lonnie, who smiled and kept coming.

She stood and tucked the book under one arm and fiddled with her hair, trying to put things in order. Did Lonnie really go out of his way to ride past when she was outside or standing at the window, cooking?

The other hands didn't ride past half so much.

She hoped he'd been doing it on purpose. Lonnie was so nice and friendly, and she liked his smile and thought he was the handsomest boy she'd ever seen.

Truth be told, she'd never really considered other boys handsome. Not the way she did Lonnie.

But then again, Lonnie didn't seem like a boy. Boys shouted and hit and pinched and tugged your braids and were always running around like dogs chasing their tails.

Lonnie was manly. He was already taller than most men, sat a horse like a man, and had big hands and a deep voice. He seemed calm and sweet and strong, things she had never, ever noticed in a boy before.

And because of this, Lonnie made her feel different, too. She was no longer a girl, seeking solely the company of other girls.

Suddenly, she felt like a young woman, and she very much enjoyed the brief exchanges they shared. She wanted more time with him and wanted him to see her not as a girl but as a woman.

But today, even more than before, she was excited to see him because she had something for him tucked in her apron pocket.

Oh my goodness, she thought with a wave of embarrassment. *I'm still wearing my apron!*

She had taken such care with her dress and hair this morning… and now she was wearing her silly old apron.

She wished she could turn back time and take off her apron, as she had planned, but Lonnie was here now, his long, golden hair shining in the sun as he tipped his hat and smiled and said in that deep voice of his, "Good morning, Miss Katie."

"Good morning, Lonnie," she said, coming off the stairs, and pulling the gift from the despised apron. "Can you keep a secret?"

Lonnie drew his beautiful horse to a stop. The stallion's

muscles rippled powerfully beneath its coat, which shone like polished mahogany. The bright white diamond on its forehead added the sense of great intelligence to its physical prowess.

"I reckon I can keep a secret just as well as the next fella," he said with a grin. "What is it, Miss Katie?"

"I have something for you, but if you let the other men know, I'm afraid they'll be cross with me because I didn't set any aside for them."

She held up the bundle for him, and he leaned and took it with a smile, the fingers of his big hand brushing casually against hers.

The feel of his touch thrilled her.

Lonnie grinned down at the cloth-wrapped bundle, tilting his head quizzically. "Now, what do we have here?" he wondered aloud and unwrapped the package with his big hands.

"You said you liked my cookies," Katie blurted.

Lonnie's grin broadened into a wide smile that set her heart to fluttering. "I sure did. Thank you, Miss Katie. That was real nice of you."

"Well, you sure do work hard. I thought maybe you might get hungry. You don't have to call me that, you know."

"Call you what?"

"Miss Katie. Katie's fine."

"All right, then." He touched the brim of his hat. "I'd best be getting out there, or they'll have my hide. Thanks again for the cookies… Katie."

Off he went, riding easily in the saddle as always, like he was a part of the big stallion.

He's like a centaur, she thought, remembering the creature from *Bulfinch's Mythology*. Half man, half horse, the centaurs were wise beyond their years.

She was very thankful for their little exchange, which had gone well despite her stupidly leaving the apron on.

No sooner had this thought occurred to her than doubts flooded her mind.

He hadn't ridden past her on purpose.

He was just being nice. That's why he didn't say anything about the apron.

He thought she was a silly little girl.

He didn't even like her cookies.

Feeling a little deflated, she went back to the main house to help Mama prepare dinner for the men.

She loved working with Mama, loved when they talked and even when they didn't. Sometimes, during the silent times, Mama would hum little songs as she worked.

It was nice and reminded Katie of her own, dearly departed mother.

Later, after they finished the chili and Mama had headed out to the clothesline, Katie was cleaning up her workspace when she looked out the window and saw a pink rose sitting on the ledge.

Plucking the rose from the window ledge, she nearly squealed with delight.

There was no note, but she knew who'd left the rose, just as he knew she often stood at this window around this time.

After all, he made a point of riding past her, didn't he?

But now there was no sign of him, just the beautiful flower sitting there… for her.

All her former doubts fell away.

She held the pink petals to her nose and inhaled the sweet aroma, thinking how blessed she was.

She remembered the horrible events on the train to New York and how Mr. Bullard, now her Pa, had come to her rescue —then saved her again from her awful uncle and his horrible house woman.

The Bullards brought her here to this wonderful ranch, gave her a brother and a room, and filled that room with books.

And, she thought, breathing deeply the rose's sweet aroma, *if I hadn't come here, I never would have met Lonnie.*

Maybe it was fate.

Maybe meeting Lonnie was the main reason God had brought her here.

Turning the rose in her fingertips, she let her mind wander, as it so frequently did, into whole rose gardens of fantasy.

Maybe Lonnie loved her.

Maybe they would be married.

Mrs. Lonnie Cooper.

Her friends would still call her Katie, of course. Mrs. Katie Cooper. Or maybe by then she would be known as Kate.

Kate Cooper, a neat and tidy name. She loved the sound of it.

Lonnie could keep working the ranch and someday become foreman, and they could live in the guesthouse, and Katie could be the full-time cook, and—

"Ouch!"

She dropped the rose, her reverie broken, and stared down at the single drop of blood welling, dark and red as an ominous moon, where the thorn had pricked her finger.

CHAPTER 16

"There's some boys stirring up trouble down Texas way," Denver City Marshal Ben Travers said after handing Justice the hundred-dollar bounty for Falco.

"Texas, huh? I know somebody down there who might stand in their way."

"How's Matt doing, anyway? Heard he got shot up pretty good down in Santa Fe."

"You heard right. But he's coming along. He'll be back on the trail any day now."

It was nice, talking openly with Travers, with no need to explain or hide anything.

Nice, but strange, too.

That was one of the odd things about getting his memory back. Everything didn't come back at once. He'd see something —a face, a street, an establishment—and memories would flood his mind.

Like when he'd ridden into Denver, hunting Falco, and realized he knew Marshal Ben Travers. The men had ridden together more than once, and Travers had proven himself a man of integrity.

Which is why Justice took the marshal seriously when he said, "Matt goes after these boys, he'd best bring help."

"Who are they?"

"The Undergrove Gang. Don't know much about them. But they've hit at least two banks. They're brutally efficient. Always take a hostage, always leave bodies behind, even when they don't have to."

Justice's five-pointed scar set to itching.

Travers said, "The leader, Cyrus Undergrove, has a stack of a paper on him. He's killed a whole slew of people down through the years. He stirs up trouble, slips back over the border into Mexico, then shows up again a few months later to wreak havoc on law-abiding folks. In the past, he usually worked alone or with one or two other outlaws, but now, he's got a whole gang with him, eight or ten men, every last one of them a hardened killer."

"Thanks for the warning," Justice said. "I'll talk to my brother."

"Glad to be of service. Least I can do, what with you ridding us of Falco. You gonna be in town long, Jake? Betty and the kids will have my head if I don't invite you over."

"Thanks, Ben, but I'm leaving on the late train. Been on the trail for a bit. Looking forward to getting home to my own family."

They shook hands and parted ways.

Justice took Sixteenth Street past the railroad tracks, crossed the bridge, and soon entered the pleasant residential section on the other side of the Platte. A short time later, he arrived at the plain-looking brick house behind which he'd stabled Dagger.

Retrieving the keys he'd gotten earlier from his bank box, he opened the door and went inside. Everything was modest yet functional, a small home with little furniture, every piece of it now mantled in dust. Dust or no dust, this hidey hole was much nicer than the underground bunker he'd discovered outside Leadville.

He went to the back of the house and unlocked an iron door in the brick wall, revealing a large, windowless room lost to shadows.

He lit a coal lamp and stepped inside. Racks of rifles and shotguns stood at attention, surrounding a long table covered in revolvers and other weapons. Beneath this table and beside the rifle racks were enough boxes of ammunition to supply a small army.

After retrieving a Winchester to replace the one he'd given to Miguel Sanchez, he locked up the room and went outside to check on Dagger.

With several hours to kill before the train would arrive, he decided to walk to a saloon and have a beer or two. Then, he'd send Nora a telegraph and maybe send another to Matt and see what was up with this Undergrove Gang. After that, he'd probably get some grub.

But first, the beer.

So he walked to the Highland House on the corner of 15th and Platte. Through its open door spilled the good smells of beer and frying food and the sound of off-duty miners shouting and laughing as they guzzled their hard-won earnings.

Just outside the door, a scrawny, dark-haired, shoeless boy in raggedy clothes stared through the open door and into the bar with a look of wistful longing.

If ever a boy had wished away the years of his life, yearning to be older, this was he. But since the kid looked a little younger than Eli, he still had a long wait ahead of him before he'd belly up to the bar in the company of men.

On the ground beside him, the kid had spread out a mess of nice trout that he'd likely caught with the bamboo pole alongside them.

Spotting Justice, the boy jumped with surprise, put on his salesman's smile, and said with a thick Italian accent, "Fish for sale, mister. Fresh caught. Best fish you ever ate."

"Is that so?" Justice said, smiling down at the kid. Since arriving in Denver, he'd seen a lot of poor kids, many of them orphans or sons of widows, he assumed. The same mines that made men rich also demanded their blood tax, after all. "How much?"

"Two bits a fish, all six for a dollar," the kid said and stood there with his hands on his hips, a tough little guy ready to haggle.

"How about a dollar apiece?" Justice said, noting the kid's scrawniness and admiring his gumption. A lot of poor kids in big towns packed together and begged or stole or strong-armed what they wanted, but this kid was working to get ahead.

"Are you serious, mister?"

"Sure," Justice said, pulling a roll of greenbacks from his pocket and peeling off six bills. "I'll take the whole mess."

"Thank you very much, sir!" The kid took the money with great reverence and handed over the fish, which were strung together on a length of twine. "You can keep the stringer, mister. This is great. Mama's gonna be real happy. I can't thank you enough."

"Your daddy a miner?" Justice asked, figuring he already knew the truth.

The boy frowned. "He was. He died in a cave-in last year. It's been hard since then."

"Tell you what," Justice said. "I'm just passing through town, so I don't have any way to cook this fish. You think I could hire your mama to cook up this fish for me?"

"Sure, mister. Sure, Mama will be happy to do that. I got a little sister, Maria, so Mama doesn't get a chance to work much. She's stuck watching Maria, and I do my best to keep us in fish and a little money."

"That's a good boy," Justice said. "Show me the way."

CHAPTER 17

The kid led him across the bridge to the Bottoms, a shantytown that sprawled among the warehouses between the railroad tracks and the river. Everything here was mud and suffering.

As they passed tents and lean-tos, dirty children and women with drawn faces watched him go.

There was hunger here. Real hunger. But what could you do? Even if Justice rented a wagon and hauled in flour and sugar and meat, how long would it last? What would they do after they'd run out of free food?

The boy led him to a shabby hovel made of scrap wood and canvas. A dispirited-looking woman sat in what looked like a discarded kitchen chair, watching a little girl in a filthy dress fussing over a headless baby doll.

The mother was young, probably in her mid-twenties, but agelessly haggard and hard-looking with poverty and worry. Beneath an unruly mop of lank, brown hair, she had a broad face with a sullen mouth, but her dark, soulful eyes were nothing short of striking.

Those eyes swung up, brightened to see her son, then narrowed at Justice.

"Lorenzo, have you gotten into trouble?"

"No, Mama, this man bought my fish."

"Oh," she said, clearly confused and more than a little cautious. "That is nice."

"For a dollar apiece!" Lorenzo said.

Rather than smiling at this, the woman looked all the more suspicious. "A dollar apiece? Why?"

"I just came into some money," Justice said truthfully without explaining he'd killed for it. "And I've seen a lot of kids in the streets begging and stealing."

She shrugged. "They're hungry."

"I imagine they are. I imagine Lorenzo is, too. But instead of begging or stealing, he's out there selling fish."

She smiled for the first time. It was a faint smile as she stared at her boy. "He's always been a good boy. Good and industrious. We would starve if it weren't for Lorenzo."

The little boy puffed out his chest.

"My name's Justice."

"My name is Donata Rossi."

"Nice to meet you, ma'am. Lorenzo said you're a widow."

She nodded. "It's a hard life, but we do our best. I wish I could find regular work, Mr. Justice, I really do. I'm a good seamstress, but who will hire me looking like this?" She frowned down at her dirty dress. Then her eyes drifted to the slapped-together shelter they called home.

"If only I had understood when Luigi died. We had a little

money then and a place to stay. Things were good. But when my husband died, I was so upset I didn't think straight. Instead of getting a job and saving money, I wallowed in grief. We spent our money, the apartment, and now…" She spread her hands, indicating her home, her children, her life.

"Do you have someplace you could go?" Justice asked. "If you had tickets, I mean. Is there someone who would take you in?"

The woman shook her head. "Not even in Italy. My parents are dead, and Luigi's parents are destitute. There is no one."

"If you did have a good job, do you have someone who could watch the children?"

"I do, so long as the job paid enough for me to give her a bit, too."

Justice nodded. "I'll be back."

"What about the fish?" Lorenzo called after him.

"Later," Justice said, and strode off across the shantytown, eating the muddy ground with his long gait.

Four hours later, he returned.

Lorenzo spotted him first and waved.

Justice waved back.

"You returned," Mrs. Rossi said, sounding surprised.

"Yes, ma'am. You folks gather up your things and come with me."

The children were instantly excited. Mrs. Rossi looked suspicious again. "Where are you taking us?"

"To get you and the children some clothing."

A brief smile lit her face then faded back into this world of mud and suffering. "That's a very kind offer, Mr. Justice, but honestly, we need food and a real roof over our heads more than we need clothing." Once again, she frowned down at her filthy garments. "It is not possible to keep anything clean here."

"Well, like you said, you'll need nice dresses for your new job."

"What job?"

"I spoke with Mr. Molloy over at Molloy's Dress Shop, and he's willing to pay you a dollar a day to work for him. Says he'll up that if you show yourself to be a good worker. Seems like a good man. I take him at his word."

For a few seconds, Mrs. Rossi just stared at him. "You're serious?"

"Serious as a stampede, ma'am. Now come on, gather your things. You won't be coming back."

"But this is our home."

"Not anymore, it isn't. Let me show you your new house."

"New house?"

"That's right. It's small and dusty and doesn't have much furniture now, but we'll get you what you need."

Lorenzo cheered.

His little sister, Maria, looked excited but confused.

Mrs. Rossi arched one brow. "Whose house is it?"

"It was mine until I hired a lawyer to draw up new papers. Now, it's yours." He handed her the deed.

As her eyes flicked over the top sheet, an incredulous smile lit her face. "But why?"

"I want to help you. Maybe someday, after you get back on your feet, you'll have the chance to help somebody else, too. Now, if you'll look at the last page, you'll notice an odd provision. You may not, under any circumstances, open the iron door at the back of the house."

"Why?"

"I have some things in there, ma'am."

"Are they dangerous?"

"Not to you. I will return at some point and retrieve them, and then the whole house will be yours. Agreed?"

"But how will we repay you?"

"I guess I'm not making myself clear, ma'am. You won't repay me. I'm giving you the house."

Mrs. Rossi just blinked at him, stunned by his generosity.

"Just say thanks, Mama!" Lorenzo chimed.

Finally, Mrs. Rossi's walls came down. Streaming tears, she clasped Justice's hands in both of hers and went to her knees, giving thanks over and over.

"Please don't do that, ma'am."

All around, folks were watching. It was downright uncomfortable.

Finally, Justice pulled her gently to her feet.

He led the overjoyed family to the little brick house across the river. The children cheered, realizing they had a home of their own. Mrs. Rossi slumped into a chair and broke down sobbing then clutched the frightened children to her bosom, assuring them that everything was okay and thanking Justice and praising God for His mercy.

Justice said, "I'll step outside while you and the children get cleaned up, ma'am. Then we'll go buy some clothing, and after you get changed, I'll introduce you to Mr. Molloy. If we move quickly, we should have time for supper at the 16th Street Café before I catch my train and go home to my own family. I noticed the café has sarsaparillas. What do you say, Lorenzo and Maria, would you like supper and a sarsaparilla?"

CHAPTER 18

Evenings after eating supper and cleaning the dishes, Katie enjoyed sitting on the porch and reading while Mama helped Eli with math and got him ready for bed.

Tonight, she was so absorbed in *Heidi*, she didn't even register the sound of the approaching horse.

"Good evening, Katie," a deep voice said.

Katie looked up from the page and blushed to see Lonnie smiling down at her. She overturned the open book on her lap, completely forgetting *Heidi* for the moment.

"Good evening, Lonnie."

"Mind if I get down and talk a moment."

"Please do."

He dismounted and dropped the stallion's reins to the ground.

"Aren't you going to hitch him?"

"Oh, Gallo's plenty hitched."

Katie grinned at that. "*Gallo*? Doesn't that mean chicken in Spanish?"

Lonnie walked over and leaned against the post, just a foot away from her. My, but he was tall.

And so handsome.

"Close," he said. "Means rooster. And there's a big difference between roosters and hens."

For some reason she couldn't quite fathom, her face burned again.

"That there horse, he's the finest cattle horse you ever seen. Wild bred, wild born. Got him in Texas. Me and these old boys I used to ride with, we came upon a herd and drove 'em into a box canyon and closed it off, and I saw this mustang and roped him straight away."

"That must have been quite exciting," Katie said, Lonnie's story transporting her even more than the pages of a book.

"Well, he sure made it interesting. You never saw a stallion fight like him. That's how he got his name. One of the vaqueros, this good ol' boy named Fredo, he said the horse had more fight in him than a rooster, and that was true, so I reckoned Gallo was a good name for him."

Katie laughed. "That's a wonderful story, Lonnie. I'll bet you have a lot of wonderful stories, living as a cowboy."

Lonnie nodded. "Some. But mostly it's just work, you know? Sweat and mud and a little blood if you ain't careful. Speaking of stories, I sure do admire the way you read so much. You sure do read a lot."

"Oh yes, I do love reading. I even reread most books. Some, I've read several times. My favorite is Great Expectations by Charles Dickens. I don't own the book, but I keep borrowing

Mr. Mueller's copy because it's so good. The characters are simply wonderful."

She had been on the verge of describing the characters when she came to her senses and blushed, embarrassed to be gushing like a little girl.

But Lonnie only smiled. "Makes a man wish he could make sense of all them squiggly marks."

"You can't read?"

Lonnie shook his head. "No, ma'am. Ain't had the time or the opportunity. Ma and Pa died when I was just little."

"I'm an orphan, too."

He looked at her for a second, his features softening with new compassion. "I thought…"

"Mr. and Mrs. Bullard adopted me last year. They're wonderful."

"They seem it. Comanches adopted me."

It was all Katie could do not to gasp. "They did?"

Lonnie nodded. "Lived with them a few years before two companies of bluebellies ambushed us. Hit us from both sides. I got shot, but I guess it wasn't time for me to die yet."

He lifted the bottom of his shirt, revealing a flat, hard-looking abdomen with a terrible scar on one side.

Katie winced. "Oh, Lonnie. I'm so sorry."

"Don't be. It healed up. And once they realized I was white, they took care of me. It was an adjustment, changing tribes again, but I sure am glad I did."

"Were the Comanches terribly brutal with you?"

"With me? Nah. They take in kids sometimes. They were strict but not brutal, not like they are with their enemies. You do not want to be captured by injuns, Comanche or otherwise. I won't tell you what they did."

She shuddered, remembering horrible stories she'd heard. She couldn't quite square this friendly young man with those terrifying savages.

"The one thing the Comanches did, they taught me horses. I mean everything. They're horse warriors, and they know everything there is to know about horses. Where to find 'em, how to break 'em, how to ride 'em. There ain't nobody better."

"That's how come you're so good at cowboying?"

He shrugged. "I love horses and love the work. The soldiers handed me off to a rancher. I was about ten, but I was tall for my age and knew more about horses than most of his cowpokes, so he threw me on a pony and put me to work. Been riding and roping ever since. Then, when I was thirteen, I left the ranch and started going on cattle drives, doing a man's work and earning a man's wages. But that's why I can't read."

"I'll teach you to read," Katie blurted impulsively.

Lonnie surprised her then, blushing. He dropped his eyes for a second. "I appreciate the offer, Katie." His hazel eyes throbbed with sincerity. "I surely do. But it would never work. I'm too dumb to read."

"Too dumb? The way you work, why, you must be way smarter than me!"

"Heh. You don't need a strong mind to work, Katie. All you need is a strong back and two strong hands and maybe some grit in here." He patted his chest.

"Lonnie Cooper, you can't believe that. You are clearly an intelligent man. Knowing all you know. You ride beautifully. You break mustangs better than anyone I ever saw."

"That's the Comanche in me."

Katie hesitated briefly, not liking the notion of what he'd said, of some savage strain still living in him; but her heart was on a mission, and she stood and fixed him with her most determined look. "I am going to teach you to read, Lonnie Cooper, and that's all there is to it. I insist." She stomped her foot for emphasis.

Lonnie laughed. It was a wonderful sound, deep and musical. "Well, if you insist, I reckon I have to at least give it a try. But don't get your hopes up, Katie. I ain't nothing but a dumb old cowboy."

"Oh no you're not. And I'm going to prove it to you."

He nodded. "All right then. I sure appreciate you taking an interest, and I hope you ain't too disappointed when you see how little I got between my ears. In the meantime, I wanted to let you and Mrs. Bullard know what I'm doing tomorrow."

"It's your day off, Lonnie," Katie said, secretly wishing they could spend it together and have a picnic or something like people sometimes did in books. "You don't have to ask."

"Oh, I know. I just thought maybe, well, if you and your mama and Eli wasn't doing nothing, maybe y'all might like to come."

She was thrilled at the suggestion, vague as it was. "What is it?"

"They're having a cowboy competition over in Dos Pesos. Roping and riding, such as that. The winner gets thirty dollars."

"That much?"

"Yes, ma'am. And I'm fixing to win. I might not be much at book reading, but I can ride."

"Oh, I'd love to come, Lonnie. I hope Mama says yes."

Lonnie smiled brightly at her. "I hope so, too, Katie."

"Oh, and I just remembered. Pa should be home tomorrow. He sent a telegram saying so. I'm sure he'd love to watch, too."

"That would be great. I'm looking forward to meeting your pa. Everybody says he's quite the man."

"He is the greatest man I've ever met," Katie said, but added silently to herself, *except maybe for you, Lonnie.*

CHAPTER 19

On his way home, Justice stopped at the Contreras ranch to check on the pups. He'd been gone longer than expected and figured the pups were more than ready.

As he neared the house, a pair of small, multi-colored blurs shot from the bushes to nip at Dagger's shanks. The unflappable stallion brought his hooves down hard and nearly settled the matter then and there.

The puppies retreated a short distance and stood there, heads low, tongues lolling, eyes gleaming like little furnaces.

They were huge. He'd never seen such large pups. And judging by their furry bear paws, they were still gonna get a lot bigger.

Justice shook his head. He should've tied Rafer up.

What in the world was he gonna do with a couple of spirited young wolfdogs?

Reaching the house, he got down.

The pups trotted over with the wary interest half-wild dogs have for strong men.

"You two leave my horse alone, or I'll shoot you," he told them.

The dogs sat, looking up at him with those gleaming eyes and smiling mouths. He noticed one of them had a white chin. Otherwise, they were both patchier than calicos.

The door opened, and a smiling Diego emerged from the house. "It's about time. I assume you're here to take those devil dogs off my hands."

"I reckon so. I was hoping I'd get here, and they wouldn't look at all like Rafer, but…"

"Yeah, there's no denying their parentage. Talk about spitting images. It's like they didn't even have the decency to consider their mama's bloodline."

"These are the males, then?"

"Oh yeah. The females are smart enough to stick with their mama. Got them in the barn, hoping you'd show up and take these monsters away. They come back here, I'm giving them both barrels."

Justice could tell by Diego's smile that he was joking but also understood that he now officially had his hands full.

Dagger snorted and stomped, and Justice turned to see the white-bearded pup skitter away.

The door opened again, and a very pregnant young woman waddled out onto the porch. She looked like an eighteen-year-old Eugenia.

"Justice," Diego said, "this is my youngest daughter, Marta."

Justice swept the hat from his head and said it was nice to meet her, and Marta smiled and said the same.

They talked briefly, then Diego's daughter retreated into the house.

"Marta and her husband, Guillermo, are visiting for a week," Diego explained, then raised one silver eyebrow. "Guillermo was one of those suitors I mentioned."

"Hmm," Justice said, picturing the woman's swollen belly. "I appreciate the warning. Luckily, Katie cares a lot more about books than boys. Besides, she's not exactly a social butterfly, living out here with us. I doubt she has any interest in old Clem."

"Well, you just keep an eye," Diego said sagely. "These suitor types, they have a way of sniffing out young ladies."

"All right. Well, what are we gonna do about these pups?"

"*We?* You got a prairie dog in your pocket? They're your problem now, my friend."

"I was afraid you were gonna say that." Justice turned to the dogs, who wrestled in a colorful blur of dust and snapping teeth.

He whistled sharply.

The dogs stopped fighting and blinked at him.

He crouched down. "Here."

The dogs wriggle-walked to him, tails tucked and bright eyes snatching glances before quickly looking at the ground again.

He reached out and grabbed the one with the white beard, got his hands under the dog's front legs, and held him out at arm's length, staring into his eyes.

He was a heavy thing.

The dog struggled briefly, growling, then averted his eyes and quit fighting.

Justice turned him from side to side, examining the shape of his skull. He was Rafer's spitting image, anyway, right down to the big bump on his head.

He put the dog down and grabbed his brother, who immediately latched onto Justice's thumb with a mouthful of needle teeth.

It smarted, but Justice had the sense not to holler or try to shake free. He lifted the dog, staring into his eyes, and a second later, the pup drooped in his hands and looked away.

Diego laughed. "Your thumb's bleeding, partner. Looks like maybe you've finally met your match."

"They'll mind me," Justice said. "All right, my so-called friend. I best be heading back to the ranch. I been gone a while, and Nora's much prettier than you."

"I won't argue that point. How are you fixing to get those wily critters home? You want to borrow a cart?"

"No. They'll either learn to follow me or die in the desert. It's up to them."

He climbed back into the saddle, rode a short distance, then turned and whistled.

The pups popped to their feet and followed him across the desolate range, leaving behind a laughing Diego.

CHAPTER 20

The pups followed Justice all the way to his ranch, where a larger, multicolored shape came trotting out of the brush and put them both on their backs.

"Rafer," Justice said when the pups' father stood growling over them. He doubted Rafer would kill them and suspected he might even know they were his sons, but with a dog like Rafer, it was worth saying something.

A moment later, Eli appeared out of nowhere, apparently summoned, in the manner of boys everywhere, by the arrival of puppies. He came running over, shouted his hello to Justice, and plowed straight into the pups.

Justice watched, wondering if the boy might get a bloody hand. If he did, it was on him. Justice had already told him that all guns were loaded, all horses kick, and all dogs bite.

But boys and puppies share a bond that defies all logic, and a second later, Eli was on the ground, and the pups were playfully tugging at his sleeves and pantlegs. Then the one with the white beard snatched his hat and ran off, and Eli and the other pup chased after him, making a lot of noise.

Rafer watched with a look of contempt then turned his eyes on Justice.

"Don't look at me that way, Rafer. They're your pups, not mine."

"Welcome home, Pa!" Katie said, running out, followed by a smiling Nora, who was showing a bit more in the belly. The notion sent a thrill through him. Their son or daughter was alive in there. He couldn't wait to meet the baby.

How I love this family, Justice thought, hopping down to scoop his daughter into an embrace.

A moment later, Nora reached them, and Justice took her in his arms and kissed her and said how good it was to see them all.

Nora glanced out by the barn, where Eli was chasing the pup with the hat and the other pup was leaping past the backs of his running legs, no doubt practicing his hamstringing technique.

"Well, I guess that's the last of Eli we'll see for the next few months," Nora said, and shook her head. "Boys and puppies."

"I'll say something to him."

"Well, welcome home, Mr. Bullard," Nora said and gave his arm a squeeze. "You almost missed us."

"Where are you going?"

"There's a cowboy contest in Dos Pesos today."

Justice nodded. "I saw them getting ready. Looks like quite the show. Let me take care of Dagger, and I'll go with you."

Nora smiled at that.

"I'm so glad you'll be with us, Pa," Katie said. "You can meet Lonnie, too. I think he's gonna win the whole thing!"

"Who's Lonnie?"

"Our new hand," Nora said. "I hired him in your absence. He's very good."

"Good. We can use the help. Any luck finding a cook?"

"Not yet," Nora said. "I'm still trusting the good Lord will make it clear when I cross paths with the right woman."

"Smart," Justice said.

"Mama," Katie said, "is it all right if I go back inside? I just changed my mind. I want to wear my blue ribbon instead."

"That's fine, sweetie."

"Hold on just a second, Katie. I got a little something for you on the trail."

Katie's eyes lit up as he pulled the book from his saddlebag.

Taking it, she read the title aloud. "*The Merry Adventures of Robin Hood*. Thank you, Pa! They had a copy of this in the orphanage, but the nuns wouldn't let me read it. Thank you!"

She hugged him fiercely, filling his heart with joy.

As they stepped apart, Katie said, "Wait till you meet Lonnie, Pa. You're going to really like him."

Justice felt something stir in him, something he'd never experienced before, something he didn't have a name for, something like suspicion and protectiveness all rolled into one. Instantly, he pictured a grinning Diego. "What's this Lonnie look like?" he asked. "Maybe I saw him while I was riding past."

"Oh, you'll know him when you see him, Pa," Katie said, her face lighting up even more than it had when he handed her the new book. "He's almost as tall as you with long golden hair. He's so handsome, isn't he, Mama?"

"He's a nice-looking young man," Nora conceded soberly. "More importantly, he's a very good worker."

Justice blinked at her, one of the phrases she'd just spoken stuck in his mind like a bone in a throat.

Young man.

How young?

And once again, Diego's grinning face came back to him, this time accompanied by the old rancher's words.

These suitor types, they have a way of sniffing out young ladies.

CHAPTER 21

J
ustice reckoned the cowboy contest, what some folks were
calling a *rodeo,* had been inspired by Buffalo Bill's Wild
West Show, which had just premiered the previous year.

Whatever the case, it was a chaotic affair, with several dozen
cowboys trying to prove they were the best at riding, roping,
branding steers, and wrestling bulls.

The new kid, Lonnie—Justice could never forget his name,
not with Katie saying it every few seconds—could do it all.

Justice didn't like the kid's long hair, and Katie's giddy fascination made his hackles rise, but when the announcers named
Lonnie Cooper "cowboy of the year," Justice had to admit Nora
had hired a top hand.

Perhaps the boy had a drifter's heart like so many cowboys,
Justice thought, watching as a smiling Lonnie tipped his hat to a
beaming Katie. Maybe, having won a month's salary at one go,
Lonnie would blow out of town like tumbleweed.

Justice hoped so. Yes, he would lose a good worker. But it would still be for the best.

"Isn't he wonderful?" Katie exclaimed.

"He sure is!" Eli chimed. "Mr. Lonnie's the cowboy of the year!"

"He puts the boy in cowboy," Clem remarked, "skinny as he is, but he can ride and rope. There's no denying that."

Nora squeezed Justice's arm. "Well, Mr. Bullard? Do you approve of my new hire?"

"He's a top hand," Justice said and left it at that.

The crowd cheered as Lonnie ascended the makeshift stage to receive the grand prize and a golden championship buckle.

Nearby, a weathered man in a sombrero nodded approvingly. In Spanish, he said, "I'm 87 years old. I have spent my whole life around horses. That boy is the best vaquero I have ever seen."

Lonnie waved to the adoring crowd, bringing a fresh round of applause. Then his eyes found Katie. He grinned and tipped his hat to her.

A mesmerized Katie clapped loudly, calling his name, so spellbound that she didn't even notice Justice staring at her.

Eli had climbed to the top rail to holler his appreciation, too. The boy had surprised Justice by leaving the new pups to come along. Apparently, this Lonnie character had made quite an impression on Eli, too.

If the other cowboys were sore about losing, they sure didn't show it. They gathered around Lonnie as he came down the steps, shouted their approval, hoisted him onto their shoulders, and carried him off toward the center of town, followed by a number of smiling fans.

As they carted him off, Lonnie turned and cast a look back toward Katie, shrugged, and rode on, propelled by friends and admirers.

Katie waved goodbye, fluttering a silk handkerchief overhead, then dabbed at the corners of her eyes. "Isn't he wonderful, Pa?"

"He can ride. I'll give him that."

"He's the best!" Eli chimed in. "Did you see the size of the buckle he won?"

Justice figured Lonnie was heading off to drink beer and get his ashes hauled at one of the cathouses. If so, Justice wanted to know. After all, the young man was clearly interested in Katie, and unfortunately, the attraction appeared to be mutual.

"I've gotta go see about some things," Justice told Nora. "You and the kids go on ahead to the Inn, and I'll join you presently."

Nora quirked a brow. "We could just come with you and go to the Inn together."

"No, I'd rather do this alone." He twisted halfway around and watched the whooping knot of cowboys disappear around the corner, heading for the center of town.

"Well then, Mr. Bullard," Nora said, having clearly followed his gaze, "we will leave you to it. But we're hungry, so please don't make us wait long. Sometimes, a man like you, a good man who likes to set things straight, can tackle jobs that don't need doing yet… if ever."

"All right," Justice said, realizing it was foolish to try hiding anything from his perceptive wife. "See you in a bit."

He hurried after the cowboys, gobbling the distance with long strides. It didn't take long to catch up.

The cowboys bunched up outside The Third Peso.

Justice crossed the street, pretending to ignore them, and slipped into the shadows beneath a storefront awning.

The cowboys kept laughing and tugging at Lonnie's arm, but apparently, he didn't want to go into the saloon.

Probably in a hurry to get his ashes hauled, Justice thought bitterly. He wasn't given to hiding in shadows or thinking poorly of folks, but when the virtue of a man's daughter is at stake, it hones him to a killing edge.

Lonnie stood his ground.

The cowboys finally relented, shaking his hand and sending him on his way before disappearing into the saloon to pour some whiskey on their fresh bumps and bruises.

Lonnie walked off down the street.

He's heading straight toward The Velvet Saddle, Justice thought with a curious blend of indignation and triumph.

He watched Lonnie go. The kid sure was skinny. And that hair. Why didn't he get a haircut?

Justice shook his head, picturing the kid sitting on a bed and brushing out his hair like a woman.

Well, the first time the kid got into a bar fight, he'd learn why a man is better off keeping his hair short. Some mean drunk would grab hold of those golden locks, spin him around, and throw him halfway across the saloon.

There, he'd reached The Velvet Saddle.

But what was this?

Lonnie kept walking.

Where was he going?

Justice followed at a distance, sticking to the opposite side of the street, and saw Lonnie pause outside of Mueller's Mercantile.

The boy stood in front of the door, glancing up and down the street, looking very much like someone with a guilty conscience wanting to make sure he wasn't being followed.

Then Lonnie went inside.

What was he getting?

Justice was tempted to walk in there and see, but then Mr. Mueller would say his name, and he'd end up having to talk with the kid, which he didn't want to do until he knew what Lonnie was up to.

So he just stood there in the shadows across the street, waiting to see what the boy came out with.

It took a while, but when Lonnie came back out, all he had was a stick of yellow hard candy. The skinny cowpoke stood out in front of Mueller's grinning and sucking on his candy.

Look at him, Justice thought with contempt, some part of him both relieved and annoyed that Lonnie hadn't walked out with something incriminating. *Sucking on candy like a little kid. And that hair!*

But then Lonnie's eyes fixed on him, his grin widened, and he pulled the candy from his mouth. "Mr. Bullard?"

Furious with himself, Justice raised a hand. "Lonnie, right?"

"Yes, sir," the boy said, switching the candy to his left as he crossed the street and offered his right. "I'm Lonnie Cooper, sir. Welcome home."

At least the boy looked him in the eyes when they shook, and Justice was surprised by the strength of Lonnie's grip. The kid was young and skinny as a rail, but his hand was nearly as big as Justice's and calloused with work.

"Congratulations on the competition," Justice said.

"Thank you, sir. That was fun. I guess Mrs. Bullard probably told you, sir, that she hired me on a trial basis."

"She did."

"I hope you'll be happy with my work, sir. I'd like to stay."

"I'll let you know."

"Thank you, sir. I appreciate it."

With no further ado, Justice went on down the street, feeling more rattled than he would have felt in the wake of a gunfight.

The kid hadn't gone into the saloon or the cat house, and he had apparently gone into Mueller's to buy a stick of hard candy.

And he'd been polite to boot. Talk about throwing salt in the wound.

Justice realized he'd been set to dislike the kid.

Picturing Katie's innocent face all lit up as she watched Lonnie at the rodeo, Justice reckoned he'd been set to do more than dislike the kid. He'd been hoping to catch him at something and send him packing.

No such luck. Not yet, anyway. So far, the kid seemed all right.

But that hair.

He'd just keep an eye on him.

These were his thoughts as he moseyed into the telegraph station and learned that he had a telegram waiting on him. It was from Doc, sent three days earlier.

Jake Bullard, Dos Pesos, New Mexico (Stop) Come see me at your earliest convenience (stop) Need you in Texas (stop) Plan on spending two or three weeks here (stop) Doc

CHAPTER 22

J ustice folded the telegram, tucked it in his pocket, walked down the street, and joined his family at the Dos Pesos Inn, saying nothing about Doc's orders, not wanting to spoil their lunch.

Though, judging by the kids' excitement over Lonnie's win, nothing could have upset them then.

On the ride home, he broke it to them. He'd been wrong about the kids. In fact, he was surprised by how saddened they both were.

"I hate to leave you, I really do," he said truthfully, "but duty calls."

Nora, tough as always, disguised her disappointment. "Well, maybe you can take a nice, long break when you get home."

Later that night, after the kids went to bed, Justice and Nora sat alone at the table, talking quietly together, as was their custom.

Only tonight, Nora was doing almost all the talking. Justice couldn't help it. He just kept thinking about Lonnie and Katie and the fact that he had to up and leave again.

"What's ailing you, Mr. Bullard?"

"What do you mean?"

"You know perfectly well what I mean. You've been growling all day, and you've barely spoken two words all night. May I guess at what's bothering you?"

"I'd rather you didn't."

"All right, then," she said, suppressing a smile. "Well, I sure do wish I'd hired a cook."

"You having a hard time keeping up?"

"No, not with Katie's help, but I sure would like to go with you to Texas and visit Mother and see Faith and Luke and hear how marriage is treating them."

"That would be real nice. Isn't there someone in Dos Pesos you could hire at least for a short term? I'd love to have you and the kids along."

Nora's face lit up. "That's it, Justice. The kids."

"Huh?"

"You've given me the best idea. We can go to Texas together and bring Eli but leave Katie to take care of the house. She would enjoy cooking for the men and—"

"Absolutely not," he interrupted. "If you think I'm going to leave her alone with that sly, longhaired cowpoke…"

Nora giggled.

"Wait a second," Justice said, understanding. "You were having a little fun with me, weren't you?"

Nora nodded. "Yes, I was. I apologize. But if you won't talk to me about what's irking you, what am I supposed to do?"

"All right, then. Yes, that's what's irking me. She's just a girl."

"She's sixteen, Justice."

"You know what I mean."

"I know what you're feeling. I feel it, too. She's still a helpless little girl to us. I'm guessing maybe she always will be to one degree or another."

"Well, what about this Lonnie character? How old's he?"

"He just turned seventeen."

He chewed on that for a second. "You think he has designs on Katie?"

"I do."

"And she feels the same way?"

"She does."

"What are we gonna do about it?"

"I don't know. What did you have in mind?"

"I was thinking maybe I'd shoot him."

Nora rubbed her chin, pretending to think about it. "That might be a tad extreme, Mr. Bullard. He seems like a very nice boy."

"Nice or not, he's a cowboy."

"So?"

"Cowboys have hearts like tumbleweeds. He might get Katie all excited then drift on down the road in a week or two."

"Sounds like wishful thinking to me."

"Not hardly. I do not want to see Katie get hurt."

"I know, Justice. It's hard."

"All I'm saying is cowboys' heads are full of romantic notions. They read too many dime novels."

"Not Lonnie. He can't read."

"Can't read? How could a girl like Katie, a girl who loves to read more than anything else, even talk with some longhaired drifter who can't read?"

"Seems they talk very easily despite their differences. Besides, Katie's teaching Lonnie to read."

"Teaching him to read? When? Where? I'll just bet he's—"

"Relax, dear husband," Nora laughed. "She teaches him a bit each evening after dinner. They sit together on the front porch in plain view. Everything is very innocent, I assure you."

"Well, you just keep an eye on that kid. I don't trust him."

"I will. And for what it's worth, I do trust him. As much as a woman can trust any young man trying to lasso her daughter's heart."

"Well, I do trust you, Nora. I trust you more than anybody in the whole world, and as hard as it is for me to leave now, I know you'll take care of things here. I'm awful thankful to have such an intelligent, capable wife."

Nora slid her hand across the table and laid it atop his. "Oh, do keep going, Mr. Bullard," she joked. "I'd really like to hear more."

"We'll be here till midnight next Thursday if you want me to list everything I love about you, Nora. But truly, thank you. I know I can count on you to keep an eye on Katie and this… suitor."

Diego's word had finally sprung from his mind out of his mouth. He didn't like the taste of it.

"There is one thing that concerns me about Lonnie," Nora said.

Justice sat up straighter. "What's that?"

"Something Katie told me. The reason he's so good with horses. He was raised by Comanches."

"Comanches?" As it would with any Texan, the word put Justice instantly on edge.

Nora nodded. "You should see him break a mustang, Justice. I've never seen anything like it. I mean, it doesn't even seem possible. It's like he's using magic or something."

Justice shook his head. "Comanches. How old was he when he left them?"

"I don't know. I can ask Katie. Pretty young, I think. He said he's been riding cattle drives for a while."

"Yeah, well, that could just be the Comanche way of saying he's been rustling cattle. I'm gonna see what I can find out about this kid. In the meantime, you keep an eye. And if you end up having to fire him, keep your Webley handy and put everyone on high alert. If there's one thing every Texan knows, it's you don't want to be on the receiving end of Comanche vengeance."

CHAPTER 23

A few days later, when Justice reached Austin, he was ready for action. The whole ride in from New Mexico, he'd been stewing over Lonnie and Katie and wondering why Doc needed him. Must be something important for Doc to tell him to hurry.

He walked down Congress Avenue past the capitol, looking forward to putting this mystery to rest and getting busy doing whatever Doc had in store for him, but something he saw made him lurch to a stop.

A short distance ahead of him, a small boy was looking into a shop window and walked straight into a vendor's cart of flowers.

The cart rocked. Flowers swayed. The boy fell backward.

"Are you all right?" the startled florist wanted to know.

But the boy's father, a big, beefy man with a cockeyed bowler's cap, red suspenders, and his sleeves rolled up, grabbed the boy by the arm, hauled him to his feet, and cuffed him hard in the back of the head, making the boy stagger. "Watch where you're going, stupid!"

Seeing the man strike the small boy so hard made Justice angry. But what really set his five-pointed scar to burning was what he saw in the faces of the man's wife and daughter.

They looked terrified for the boy and likely for themselves, judging by the black eyes they both sported.

Figuring he'd taken measure of this man, Justice moved forward. "Make you feel tough, hitting women and children?"

The man turned swiftly in Justice's direction. An ugly scar ran the length of one jowl, as pale against his angry red face as a dead worm draped across a ripe tomato. The man puffed out his chest. "If you weren't wearing them gun belts, I'd hit you instead, big mouth."

"Pardon me, ma'am," Justice said to the shocked florist. "Would you mind holding my gun belt for a moment? It won't take long."

The lady nodded wordlessly, and Justice calmly removed his double holster, keeping an eye on the man, who seemed like the sort to pounce when he thought he had an advantage.

But the man merely rolled his big shoulders and grinned like he'd won a free cake. "Come on, then, and I'll blacken your eyes just like I blackened theirs."

The man shuffled forward, his big hands balled into fists.

After the frustration of recent days, Justice wanted to wade in there and trade with this big bully, but that would be irresponsible. So he tamped down his anger and went to work, jerking to one side when the man started hurling haymakers.

To the man's credit, he threw punches in bunches, coming at

Justice with several looping shots, grunting with effort, putting everything into it.

Justice moved away at an angle, looking for a clear opening.

The man was already breathing hard. "You gonna dance or fight, coward?"

He drove forward again, swinging for Justice's body.

Timing the charge, Justice threw a ripping right uppercut, nailing the man under the chin and jerking his head back, then followed up with a crushing left hook that caught the man on the point of his jaw, spun his head sharply, and dropped him to the street.

Instantly, the man struggled onto all fours, roaring with anger.

So the guy could take a punch. Which meant this could go on and on. Which also meant Justice might break his knuckles putting this guy down for good.

Meanwhile, he would likely be needing his hands in good working order for whatever Doc wanted him to do.

So rather than letting the man get to his feet again, Justice stomped down between his shoulder blades, knocking him flat, then jumped on top of him and quickly seized the man's jaw and hair in his powerful hands and twisted, making the man curse and bellow.

"One quick twist," Justice told him, "and I could snap your neck. Kill you instantly. Make the world a better place."

"Don't," the man begged.

"It would be so easy," Justice said, "but would it be right? It's a thing I've asked myself many times. A poor family like yours, are they better off with you or without you? Should I kill you and save them the beatings? Or would their lives be even harder without you? I can only do so much. Then I have to move on. But I sure hate to think of you hurting them."

"I won't do it again."

"You won't, huh?"

"No. Honest."

"What's your name?"

"Asa Plum."

"Where do you live, Asa?"

The man gave him an address in Austin.

Still gripping the man's hair and chin, Justice said, "Tell you what, Asa. I'm on my way to see a man, and I'm going to give him your name and address."

"Okay. Just don't snap my neck. I won't—"

"Shh, Asa. I'm talking now. Listen. You'll want to hear this."

"All right."

"This man, he's like me, except he's not so philosophical. He's what you might call a realist. See, if you'd taken a swing at him, you'd already be dead. He wouldn't waste time chatting with you. He'd just snap your neck and be done with it. Do you understand?"

"Yeah."

"Now, you promise you're not gonna hurt your family anymore?"

"I promise."

"You'd better not, because I'm going to ask this man to check in on your family from time to time."

"I won't hurt them ever again."

"Then you will never even notice my friend. You might even start to doubt he exists. But if he sees any black eyes or split lips…"

"He won't! That ain't never gonna happen again, I swear."

"I hope so, Asa, but he'll be watching. And one thing's for sure, if you do hurt them, you won't do it ever again."

Onlookers eyed Justice warily as he released the battered bully, retrieved his gun belt, thanked the florist, and walked on down the street.

CHAPTER 24

"How does it feel, being back on the trail?" Doc asked once they'd moved from his barber shop and telegraph office into the back room from which he controlled the activity of silent justices.

"Feels good."

"It's what you're meant for, Jake. It's who you are."

"I did a lot of thinking about that over the winter. When Rose shot my badge off, I thought, now I gotta figure out who I really am."

"And you've done that?"

"More or less. I gotta say being back out on the trail has stirred up some uncomfortable realizations."

"You miss your family."

"I do."

"That's one reason why silent justices aren't allowed to marry. A man dreaming of home might miss something, might even get himself killed."

"That won't be a problem. When I'm on the job, I'm on the job."

Doc nodded at that. "Another problem with family is leaving them alone. To help others, you have to leave your own family without your protection."

"That does bother me some."

"Is it a problem?"

"I'll handle it. My recent realizations don't have anything to do with my family."

Doc leaned back in his chair and tented his fingers, his intelligent eyes twinkling with almost predatory interest. "Explain."

"I guess it's about the scope of our job, the limitations."

Doc nodded. "We'll never stop all the bad men."

"That's part of it. Lately, it's the good folks bothering me."

"Your inability to make their lives right again?"

"Yes, sir."

"You always were compassionate, Jake. It's what makes you such a good silent justice. You're a study in contrast, a stone-cold killer of bad men whose heart bleeds for the downtrodden."

"I do what I can out there, but the streets are full of widows and orphans and the shadows are full of thieves and murderers. For everyone I help, there are thousands and thousands who also need a hand, folks I'll never even meet."

Doc spread his hands. "We do what we can do, and it's all we can do. Truth be told, I think there are a lot of people out there feeling similar frustration. That's the price of helping others. When you stick to your own, maybe just help a neighbor here and there, you keep the troubles of the world at bay. You get busy with your own life and stay busy and that's that. But once you start helping folks, you can't help but notice how many other folks need help."

Justice nodded, sensing the truth in Doc's words.

"What you're struggling with," Doc said, "isn't so much a limitation of our work, Jake, as it is a limitation of life. Reminds me of the ancient Chinese curse, *May you live in interesting times.*"

Justice chuckled. "That's a pretty good curse."

"It is. And you are finding your time on the trail interesting."

"Yes, sir. Very interesting."

Doc smiled. "You know, I had an almost identical conversation with your father several years ago."

"You did?"

"I did. And when I mentioned the curse, he laughed just like you did."

"I miss him, sir."

"I'll bet you do. We all do. And I still need to fill his position. Your father's murder left a gaping hole in the ranks of the silent justices."

"You have a replacement in mind?"

"I have candidates. One reason I wanted you here today was to ask you about a couple of them."

"They're men I know?"

"They are. I would also consider your cousin Luke if he hadn't gotten married."

"He's a good man," Justice said, but felt instant relief that Luke would not be considered. After all, what would happen to Faith if Luke got killed?

Before Justice could work out the irony of that line of thought, Doc said, "What do you know about Elijah Rable?"

"Lije is a good man. Quick on the draw, too. Real quick. Cool head, lots of sand." He nodded, thinking about it. "It'd be hard to find a better man."

"A short time ago, he handled quite a big problem over in Destitution."

"I heard something about that. Lots of folks involved."

"Lots. But your friend took care of business. Only trouble is, I hear he rode off with a girl. You haven't talked with him?"

"No, sir. Not word one."

Doc nodded thoughtfully. "If he's hitched his wagon to this woman, that disqualifies him. Otherwise, I believe he might be our man."

"You said there was another candidate?"

"Yes. More than one, in fact. But one more that you know. Would you care to guess?"

It only took a second. "Coronado."

"That is correct. He seems to have performed well during your ill-advised vacation in Mexico."

"He's tough as nails. Good shot, keeps his head when the lead's flying, plenty of sand. But he's still pretty banged up from our time down there."

"You think he could hold up on the trail?"

"I don't know. Also, if I'm honest, sir, I have some doubts. You won't find a better man, but I'm not sure he'd even want to ride alone, doing what we do."

"I'd wondered that. If he heals up, I might have you talk to him about it."

"Happy to do it, sir. Like I said, he's a good man."

"Speaking of healing, the main reason I called you here was to talk about Matt."

"What about Matt?" Justice said, feeling the protectiveness any man feels for his brother. "Everything okay?"

"As far as I know. Matt says he's good as new. He wants to get back on the trail. But that was a major injury he sustained."

"Yes, sir. In this line of work, major injuries come with the territory. You're not letting him go, are you?"

"No. Quite the opposite. I want to make sure we don't lose him. He says he's fully functional, and perhaps he is, but I don't want him riding alone into a lead storm if his shoulder remains compromised."

"If Matt says he's good, he's good."

Doc smiled at that. "You Bullards."

"Yeah, us Bullards."

"Here's the thing, Jake. There's a mess south of here that needs cleaning up. It's a job for more than one man."

"And you want me and Matt to take care of it?"

"That's right. It'll get Matt back on the trail and let him test that shoulder."

"When do we leave?"

"At your leisure."

"Soon, then."

"Yes, it's a situation that needs fixing. Until you take care of it, people will suffer."

"Interesting times we live in."

"Yes, very interesting." Doc handed him a pair of folders. "The top folder contains everything you need to know. Should make for entertaining reading on the long coach ride to Fredericksburg."

"All right. And the other folder?"

"Details on a group of bank robbers called the Undergrove Gang."

"I just heard about them."

"They have people talking. Bad bunch. Big and capable. They're not like other gangs. They're smart and brutal. Unlike most criminals, they are organized and methodical."

"Which makes them dangerous."

"Yes."

"How come we aren't going after them, then?"

"Because they slipped over the border into Mexico. It's what they do. Come over here, rob a bank, kill some folks, and then flee the country. And no, before you ask, you can't go after them. If you cross the border again, the commander will boil us in the same pot."

"Hey, it all worked out down there. We freed a lot of women on both sides of the border."

"Which is why you and I aren't already simmering in that pot. No, we'll just have to wait for the Undergrove Gang to come north again. I don't think we'll need to wait long. So read the information and stay ready."

"Yes, sir."

"Now, if you have everything you need, Jake, I have an appointment to cut hair in ten minutes."

"All right. I'll clear out of here. I did have one favor to ask, though, sir."

"What's that?"

Justice pulled the train ticket from his pocket and borrowed one of Doc's pens, wrote on the stub, and handed it to his supervisor.

Doc read the words. "Who is Asa Plum?"

CHAPTER 25

Judging by his wanted poster, Cyrus Undergrove was an ugly cuss with a squat face held up by a heavy jaw bristling with black stubble. The paper on him combined to a staggering amount, almost seven thousand dollars, meaning every bounty hunter in the Southwest would be trailing his hide.

They'd need luck.

After reading the report, Justice understood that Undergrove was as cautious as he was brutal. He put his own safety first, always took a hostage, and never hesitated to kill if it might increase his odds of survival. One of his men, Hank Hardesty, came into town before each job, scaled atop a building in view of the bank, and acted as a sniper, ensuring Undergrove's escape.

Justice memorized faces and facts of each gang member, nine in all. They were all hard men, and every one of them had hiked prior to throwing in with Undergrove.

The fact that he was getting them to work together in such an orderly fashion spoke volumes about Undergrove.

Taking him down would be a chore.

Still, Justice hoped Undergrove would come back over the border and give him a chance.

The stagecoach ride from Austin was long, hot, and bumpy, so when Justice finally arrived in Fredericksburg, he went straight to Ludwig Schmidt's hotel and had a good German beer.

Next, he stopped by Wagner's Mercantile to see how Emma and Wilhelm Wagner were making out in their new venture.

Wilhelm recognized him at once and came around the counter to shake his hand. "Mr. Bullard, so wonderful to see you, sir. Emma, we have a visitor!"

Several months earlier, when Justice had met Emma Wagner on the train, she had been very noticeably pregnant. He had surrendered his Pullman berth for her comfort then helped her get from Austin to Fredericksburg, where she and her husband were risking everything to start this store.

Now, coming up the aisle with a bright smile on her face, she bounced the baby, a blue-eyed little girl with hair the color of cornsilk. "It is wonderful to see you again, Mr. Bullard."

He fussed with the baby, whose name was Wilhelmina or "Mina" for short.

They asked him all about his life, and he told them some of it. They were delighted to learn of his marriage, Nora's pregnancy, and the adoption of Katie.

Meanwhile, things had been going well for the Wagners. The store was prospering, and they were very happy.

"Please join us at our home for dinner tonight," Wilhelm said, but Justice politely declined.

"I'm heading out to my brother's ranch right after this."

"Your family and friends have given us a lot of business," Wilhelm said. "Please give Matt and Luke our regards."

Once they'd caught up, Justice moseyed over to the rack of books and instantly saw one he knew would delight Katie.

"I'm happy to see you have this in stock," he said, carrying the book to the counter. My daughter loves it, but the local mercantile never has any copies in stock."

After saying his goodbyes, Justice walked down to the livery and saw his old friend, Del Haskins.

They chewed the fat for a while, Justice remembering much more about Del now and recalling how they'd run together through childhood like a pair of hounds on a fresh track.

It was good, catching up, and Justice could see it meant a lot to Del, too.

Finally, Justice said, "I need to rent a horse. Nothing fancy. Just good enough to get me out to the ranch and back."

"Got a big buckskin gelding back there that ought to do the trick. He can be a little wily but nothing you can't handle, Jake."

When Justice tried to pay, Del shook his head.

"No can do, brother. If I told you once, I told you a thousand times, your money's no good here." He grinned. "Now, take the horse and get off my property before I throw you out."

"See, I knew you would say that. Which is why I got these for you in Austin." Justice opened his saddle bag, pulled out a box and two paper sacks, and handed them all to the hostler.

Del grinned at the box. "My favorite cigars. You remembered."

"Yeah, my memories are coming back."

"Seems like it. What's in the bags?"

"Open them and find out."

As Del peered into each bag, his smile grew and grew. "Tea and biscuits. My favorites. Thanks, Jake. Now, I feel bad for not loaning you a better horse!"

As Justice had assumed, there was nothing wrong with the gelding. He was a big horse, fit Justice well, and showed none of the wiliness Del had mentioned.

Even when, halfway to the ranch, two hooded men jumped out from behind some roadside live oaks and started shouting and pointing weapons at Justice, the horse remained calm.

CHAPTER 26

With a calm surpassing even that of the sedate gelding, Justice remarked, "Well, I have to say it's a surprise to meet highwaymen on the outskirts of a nice, peaceful town like Fredericksburg."

Both young men wore scarves across their faces.

The shorter of the pair poked his muzzle at Justice. "Shut up, mister, and get down off that horse. He's our horse now."

Justice dismounted slowly. "You boys sure you want to do this? Folks don't cotton to horse thieves around these parts."

The shorter man spoke again. "Let 'em try and catch us. Now, you go ahead and pull them shooting irons, mister. Nice and slow. That's it. Now hold 'em out backwards. That's it. Hold onto the barrels. Face the butts toward my partner.

But the other man had gone totally rigid. "Forget it. You go ahead, mister. It's your lucky day."

The other guy was confused. "What are you talking about? We got him dead to rights."

"Shut up. You go on ahead, mister." He tried to put a little bluster in his voice but just ended up sounding frightened. "Get on your horse and ride."

"Jim Bob?" Justice asked, recognizing the voice and eyes of Jericho Boon's oldest son.

The other boy's eyes swelled above his mask. "He recognized you, Jim Bob. Now we gotta shoot him."

"Is that who you've become, Jim Bob?" Justice asked softly. "A man who'd shoot a family friend?"

"No, sir. Put the gun away, Kyle."

"No can do, Jim Bob. He ain't my boss, and neither are you. If we just let him go—"

As the boy named Kyle turned to shout at his friend, Justice executed a lightning-quick border roll, flipping the outstretched Colts, snatching them by the butts, and pulling back the triggers as he shoved one muzzle into Kyle's temple and pointed the other at Jim Bob Boon.

A second later, the boys had laid their weapons on the ground and pulled down their masks.

"Don't look at your feet," Justice said. "Look me in the eyes. Now, what in the world happened to you, Jim Bob?"

Jim Bob looked at him and looked away again. "I ran out of money."

"Needing money is not an excuse for taking it from someone else."

"I know, Mr. Bullard."

"You were good with horses. Good enough to earn an honest living."

Jim Bob nodded. "I'm sorry, Mr. Bullard. If I had known it was you, I never would have even—"

"Well, then I'm glad it was me who came along and not some other poor soul… or someone who would've shot you dead. You boys do remember you're in Texas, right?"

The young men nodded, studying their boots again.

Justice shook his head. "I can smell the beer on your breath. You boys drank some liquid courage and decided you'd become outlaws, huh?"

They nodded sheepishly.

"What's your last name, Kyle?"

"Dobbs, sir."

"Dobbs? Is David your father?"

"No, sir. David's my grandpappy. My daddy's name is Parker."

"Parker's your daddy?" Justice's mind did some quick calculations. "How old are you, boy?"

"Thirteen, sir."

"Thirteen? You're a biggun, aren't you? Seems like your brain's got a lot of catching up to do with them shoulders of yours."

"Yes, sir."

Justice turned back to Jim Bob. "And what about your daddy? Does Jethro know you're out here robbing folks?"

"My daddy's dead, sir."

Something softened in Justice. Not much. But a little. "Dead? Dead how?"

"Lightning struck here a year back. Went out to call the cows one night. Storm hadn't even got there yet. But the lightning sure had. He held on for a few days. But it done for him."

"I'm sorry to hear that, Jim Bob. He was a good man. He

rode in the war with my Pa, who never had anything but praise for your daddy."

The kid nodded, suddenly looking younger than he was. Justice could see he was fighting back tears of shame.

Good. He needed to feel ashamed.

But not forever.

What he really needed was to change his ways. Otherwise, sooner or later, somebody was gonna put a bullet through his guts.

"Now, question is, what are we going to do about this, boys?"

CHAPTER 27

T he collies came off the porch all in a tumble, barking and
yipping and wagging their shaggy tails and generally
making fools of themselves as Justice hitched the gelding to the
tree outside the house and rapped on the door.

Nobody answered, so he opened the door and went inside.
"Matt? Luke?"

Nothing.

But folks had been here recently. He could see that. So he
walked on out to the barn.

There was no one inside. Even the horses were gone. Which
made sense, of course, given that it was a lovely afternoon.

They were probably out in the pasture.

Just as Justice turned in that direction, he heard the sharp
crack of what sounded almost like a small-caliber gunfire
coming from behind the barn.

An instant later, Colt in hand, he moved forward.

But before he'd taken even three steps, his mind reconsidered the sound and told him it wasn't a firearm that he'd heard.

He holstered his Colt and walked out into the corral, trailed by the collies, and saw Nora's little sister, Faith, draw back her arm and swing it forward again, making the short bull whip crack loudly.

"That's it, Faith," Luke said, smiling from atop the fence. "You're really getting it now."

"Thank you," Faith said. "This is fun."

"I see you newlyweds are working your fingers to the bone here on the ranch," Justice said, surprising them.

"Hey, Jake!" Luke said, hopping down with a huge smile on his face.

Beside him, his young wife smiled and blushed. Despite her red face, baggy work clothes, and dead eye, Nora's little sister remained gorgeous.

"Well, that's embarrassing," she said. "Bull whips aren't exactly ladylike."

"Pshaw! No Bullard ever begrudged a woman learning to handle a bullwhip… or any other weapon for that matter. Good to see you, Faith."

He pulled her into a hug, and she squeezed him back.

"Good to see you, Jake."

He let her go and shook hands with Luke, who told him Matt was next door at Agatha Barnes's house, patching the roof.

"She wanted you to fix it, of course, but we reminded her that you were in New Mexico, so she grudgingly conceded Matt to help her."

"Well," Justice laughed, "I'd best go over there and give him a hand, then. She deserves the best."

The newlyweds laughed.

"Before I head over, though, I got something for you, Faith." He reached into his pocket and pulled out the letters from Nora. He handed one to Faith, who squealed with delight.

Seeing how the other envelope was addressed, Faith said, "Want me to give that to Mother?"

"No thanks. I'd best pay respects to my mother-in-law before heading over to Mrs. Barnes's place. Is she over at your place?"

Luke nodded. "She'll be happy to see you."

"Thanks again for the house, Jake," Faith said.

"Happy to help. How's it working out for you?"

"Great," Luke said, and putting an arm around his wife, he drew her against his side. "We couldn't be happier."

"I'm glad to hear it. And Matt and I are beyond pleased that you folks decided to stay at the ranch."

Luke's grin kept getting bigger. He turned to Faith. "Can I tell him?"

She blushed again and nodded.

"We're gonna have a baby," Luke announced.

"Congratulations," Justice said, drawing Faith into another hug and shaking his cousin's hand again. "I'm so happy for you two."

They talked a bit longer. Justice was excited to tell Nora how well her sister was doing.

Then, as he started for the new house, he remembered.

"Hey, Luke, a couple boys are coming up here tomorrow. Put 'em to work, okay? Dollar a day, make 'em earn it."

"All right. Just for the day?"

"For a while, I'm hoping."

"All right. What kind of work can they do?"

"One of them, Jim Bob Boon, is pretty good with horses. The other, this boy named Dobbs, I don't know what he's good at. Don't know if he even knows. You might have to teach him."

"Boon, huh? And Dobbs? Parker Dobbs's boy?"

Justice nodded. "Name's Kyle."

"Those two have been getting into mischief lately."

Justice allowed one side of his mouth to curl upward. "Sounds like somebody else I know."

"Fair enough. I'll see what I can do."

Then, thinking of Faith, Justice said, "You don't have to, Luke. Are you comfortable having them here with your family?"

"Sure, Jake. They step out of line, I'll put them in their place."

"I reckon they're saddle broke now, but you know boys. Sooner or later, they'll test you."

"Let 'em try. I'll tell Faith to fetch the bullwhip."

Laughing, Justice walked to the new house where they and his mother-in-law now lived. It was a nice place, plenty big, with its own small barn and stable.

On his way there, he cut across the pasture, followed, of course, by the collies. All the horses except Bourbon trotted over to see him.

Justice greeted each horse, whispering softly as he nuzzled them close, then turned his attention to the sulking stallion.

Standing with his hands on his hips, Justice said, "You just gonna stand there pouting, or are you gonna come over and see me?"

Bourbon snorted and gave his thick neck a shake then took a few reluctant steps forward.

"You expect me to meet you halfway, huh?"

The stallion trotted over to meet him, but as they came together, Bourbon must've remembered that he was supposed to be grumpy because he stopped, half turning, and lowered his head as if to graze, cropping nothing but simply going through the motions.

Justice walked past the lowered head and stood shoulder to shoulder with the big stallion. The dogs sat down around him, obliviously happy that their alpha had returned.

Finally, Bourbon lifted his head and brought it around so that his neck pressed into Justice's head, knocking his hat askew, as if to say, "All right. I'm ready for you to love me up now."

Chuckling, Justice reached up and cradled Bourbon's powerful neck, telling him he was ridiculous and that he was sorry and that he promised they'd cover some miles together right soon.

Bourbon must've taken it to heart because as Justice started for the new house again, the stallion skipped around him and tossed his head like a young colt, and when the other horses tried to get close to Justice, Bourbon drove them back, staking his claim.

At the gate, Justice took the big stallion by the head and laid his forehead into Bourbon's nose, stroking him and telling him how good it was to see him again.

Then he left the pasture and knocked on the door and soon found himself in the embrace of a very happy Mrs. Taylor. "You Bullard boys come and go like weather in the Panhandle. How long are you staying, Jake?"

"Not long, ma'am. Likely just overnight. And I'll be taking my brother with me for a spell."

"I won't even ask. But please come in and tell me how my daughter and grandchildren are. Can I get you something to drink?"

Half an hour later, Justice finally extricated himself from his wonderful mother-in-law and got Bourbon saddled and rode over to Mrs. Barnes's place, where Matt was nearly finished with the roof.

Standing amidst a small army of cats and goats, the rail-thin Mrs. Barnes stared up at him, her thin frame and wild shock of white hair making her look like a dandelion that had gone to seed. Apparently, her hearing wasn't the best because she didn't even notice Justice coming up behind her. Either that or she was just focused on supervising Matt because even when the cats and goats trotted off, she continued to stare up at the younger Bullard brother.

"You sure you fixed it?" she called up to Matt.

"Yes, ma'am. It's tighter than a weasel's banjo."

"I hope so. I just wish your brother was here. Now, there's a man who knows how to work. Of course, I never would have had to ask him in the first place. He always keeps an eye on me, your brother. He's very good that way, a very good man."

Matt flashed Justice a grin. "That he is, ma'am. It's downright difficult trying to keep up with him. Well, speak of the devil. Here he comes now."

Mrs. Barnes turned and clasped her hands over her chest, smiling up at Justice. "Oh, thank heavens! I just knew you'd come home, Jake!"

Justice tipped his hat. "Ma'am. It's always a pleasure. Mind if I climb down?"

"Oh, please do, please do. I've been having a terrible time."

"I can see that, ma'am, and I'm happy to help, of course. Would you like for me to check my brother's work for you?"

"Would you mind, Jake?" She lowered her voice a touch but was also hard of hearing, so Justice was pleased to know Matt could still hear her. "He tries, bless his heart, but... you know."

Justice patted her back gently. "Yes, ma'am. I do know." He flashed a grin up at his brother, who rolled his eyes. "He tries, bless his heart, but I'll be sure to go up and check everything real good."

CHAPTER 28

Matt had done a good job, of course. He did everything well, short of impressing Mrs. Barnes.

Once the brothers wrapped up and were heading back to the ranch, they finally talked.

"Feel like helping me kill a nest of rattlers?" Justice asked.

Matt nodded. "I never met a rattler that didn't need killing. We'll bring the collies. That one with the different colored eyes is the best snake dog you ever saw."

"Snakes I'm talking about carry shotguns and chew tobacco."

"Oh," Matt said and rode in silence for a few seconds before allowing himself to grin. "In that case, the collies can stay home. When it comes to that type of snake, I reserve the fun of killing all for myself."

"Spoken like a Bullard. These boys are holed up over in Fort Worth."

"I think I heard about them. They the ones hitting card games around the Acre?"

"The very same."

"Come through the backdoor, blasting away. Heard they shot a man through the window last time."

"Heard the same thing. Shot the dealer right in the back, then came through the door and painted the walls red."

"I'll be glad to help you put them down."

"Good."

"Doc sent you, huh?"

"Yup."

"I told him I was all right."

"Yup."

"But he sent you anyway."

"There's four in this gang."

"All right. When do we leave?"

"You got any impending social engagements?"

"Not a one."

"Me neither. Save for dinner with my mother-in-law."

"She can cook."

"I know she can. Why do you think I rode in here early as I did?"

Matt laughed. "You always got everything figured out, don't you, big brother?"

"Well, not everything. Right now, I got a situation back at the ranch that's downright confounding."

"Lay it on me."

Justice had not intended to share his troubles, but that's the way it is with brothers. They ask, you talk. And, as he told Matt about Katie and this Lonnie character, Justice realized it felt good to unload his wagon.

Matt took it all in then said, "You reckon this kid's no good?"

"I don't know. I don't really know anything about him."

"Sounds like he's a good cowboy, anyway."

"Yeah, he's a top hand."

"They're hard to come by."

"Yeah, but that doesn't matter where Katie's concerned."

"I know, big brother. All I'm saying is you don't want to cut him loose for tipping his hat at her. You reckon sidling up to her?"

"I reckon so. What's worse, I reckon she's sidling up to him."

"Well, she's sixteen. Sidling's natural enough. How old's this other character?"

"Seventeen."

"Seventeen. If he's anything like you were at seventeen, you'd best keep that girl under lock and key."

"That's what I'm thinking."

"I'm just joshing with you, Jake. You think this kid's an egg sucker? Is he the sort to sneak into the henhouse when nobody's looking?"

"If he does, I'll nail his hide to the barn."

"I know that. What I'm asking is do you think he's the type?"

"I don't know. The other day, Dos Pesos had a cowboy competition. Riding, roping, that sort of thing."

"A rodeo," Matt said, nodding. "They been popping up of late. Vaqueros been having them forever, but now folks are making a big to-do out of them."

"Right. Well, this kid Lonnie won."

"The whole thing?"

"The whole thing."

"Were there many cowboys there?"

"Dozens."

Matt whistled. "Either New Mexico's short on good cowboys, or you really do have yourself a top hand."

"Kid can ride. He's got grit, too. Him and that stallion he rides, they're one in the same when the pressure's on."

"Sounds like you almost admire him."

"I could if it weren't for…"

"Yeah. But you were saying…"

"Anyway, after he won, the other cowboys packed him off to the saloon."

"Makes sense. Thirsty work, roping steers."

"But the kid didn't go inside."

Matt arched a brow. "You followed him?"

"Yes, I followed him. This is my daughter we're talking about."

"All right, then. You followed, he didn't go in. Was he in too much of a hurry to hit the bordello?"

"That's what I expected. But no. He walked right past the cathouse and into the mercantile and came back out sucking on a piece of hard candy." Justice shook his head in disgust. "He's got hair down to his shoulders."

"Nothing a good pair of scissors can't fix. Seems to me, big brother, like maybe things aren't as bad as you fear."

Justice just looked at him, figuring Matt was right. But why did he feel so much dread?

"You're right to keep an eye, of course," Matt said. "Boys will be boys, after all, but I'm sure Nora is keeping watch."

Justice nodded again.

"If I were you," Matt continued, "I would worry less about

this Lonnie character, who doesn't sound that bad, and more about unnecessarily giving Katie's first romance both barrels. You overreact now and kick this kid off the ranch, how do you think she'll react?"

"Cry her eyes out."

"For starters, yeah, but she's a sixteen-year-old girl, Jake. This sort of thing is as natural to her as fighting was to us back then."

Justice nodded. "She doesn't seem sixteen to me."

"Well, that won't stop her from being sixteen or acting her age. You stomp this boy for liking her, how do you think she'll react when the next cowboy comes along with a twinkle in his eye?"

Justice nodded but said nothing, knowing Matt was right but not wanting to put that into words. Instead, he said, "All right. That's enough about that. Let's get back to the ranch and rustle up some top-notch grub. The sooner we get back to killing bad men, the better."

CHAPTER 29

Mary Griffin sat at her window, doing her best to look interested.

Sometimes, it was difficult to feign interest, especially with certain customers. On those days and with those customers, Mary smiled and nodded, but her mind was full of daydreams.

Now was such a time.

As Mrs. Haverly went on about her sister back in Iowa, the one whom she was wiring five dollars, Mary imagined herself just getting up without so much as a "Pardon me," deserting her station, and walking straight out of the bank.

She would never do that, of course, and couldn't afford to, not with two little ones at home and her husband laid up after falling off the ladder at work.

But it was nice to dream, especially when facing customers like this.

"Sometimes," Mrs. Haverly said, leaning close, apparently

oblivious of the line of folks waiting behind her, "I suspect my sister is exploiting my kindness. I really do. Why, the last time I visited—"

The door banged open, and a gang of armed men strode in, led by a short, squat, sneering man in a wide sombrero, who spat a smoking cigar onto the floor and announced, "We have come here to relieve you of your money!"

Oh my goodness! Mary thought, reeling backward with horror. *These were the men! The ones her manager had been warning them about. The Undergrove Gang!*

A split second later, the bank erupted in gunfire.

It started when Daniel Prather, who had been standing patiently behind Mrs. Haverly, went for his sidearm.

Mary had known Daniel since childhood. They'd gone to school together. Today, she'd been looking forward to talking to him and hearing about his pretty wife and their little ones, but no sooner had his hand moved than the gunfire exploded, and Daniel fell to the ground in a red mist.

After that, Mary didn't know what happened. In a wild panic, she dropped to the ground beneath her window and curled up in a tight ball as the shooting went on and on and people screamed and hollered, and where oh where was Sheriff McCarthy?

When the shooting stopped, the voice of the man in the sombrero said, "Next one of you who screams gets what they got. The bank manager has three seconds to get out here with his hands up."

Further down the line, teller Violet Chambers spoke in a trembling voice. "The bank manager's dead, sir. That's him lying on the floor."

Cursing, the man in the sombrero told Violet to get the keys off Mr. Haggerty's body.

All the while, Mary's mind reeled with terror. Mr. Haggerty was dead?

That wasn't possible…

Out in the street, a big rifle boomed. A Sharps, by the sound of it, as any girl who'd grown up in this hide-hunting territory would know.

"Everybody in the vault," the man in the sombrero demanded, and Mary rose on shaky legs and started shuffling into the cavernous vault with her coworkers.

But the man in the sombrero pointed his pistol at her. "You. You're coming with me."

Mary touched her fingertips to the top of her blouse and tried to ask "Me?" but the word stuck in her throat.

"Yes, you. Come on."

Out in the street, the Sharps roared again. And again. And once more.

The bank robbers strode out of the bank, carrying sacks of money and dragging Mary along.

In a horrified whisper, she managed to ask, "Where?"

"Don't worry, ma'am," the man squeezing her arm in an iron grip said. "It won't be but a short trip."

He lifted her onto a horse and climbed up behind her, and suddenly, she was bouncing up and down at the heart of the galloping gang.

A few townsfolk came out and exchanged gunfire with the fleeing bank robbers. Others, spotting her, held their fire.

Then, they were out of town, charging into the badlands.

A short time later, they stopped abruptly, and the man let

her down from his horse. "Told you it wouldn't be but a short trip," he said, and raised his pistol.

"Wait," she said, raising her hands. "No!"

The muzzle flashed. Mary felt a brief, apocalyptic burst of pain, and all was darkness.

CHAPTER 30

Nora gave a slight nod of her head. "Thank you, Lonnie."
Helping her into the buggy, the boy explained, "My pleasure, ma'am. I seen you was fixing to head to town and thought since it was my day off maybe I could ride along and give you a hand with anything that needs wrangling. Also, I gotta grab something at the mercantile."

"All right, Lonnie. That would be very nice. Thank you. Do you care to drive?"

"I'd be honored, ma'am."

Well, she thought, *this is certain to be interesting.*

And sure enough, shortly after they'd started for town, Lonnie said, "Ma'am, I wanted to say I sure do admire your daughter."

Nora said nothing, letting the boy talk.

"The way she cooks, I mean, and how she reads all the time? She's awful smart, and real nice. Nobody ever taught me to read before."

"Katie is a very special girl."

Lonnie nodded, smiling. "She sure is, ma'am. She's the most special girl I ever met by a mile."

He glanced at her and looked nervously away, and they rode in silence for several seconds.

It was a curious thing to watch the muscles in his jaw bunch and loosen, to watch his big hands tighten on the reins, and to watch his eyes harden against the distance. She had never seen someone so clearly summoning courage… a curious thing indeed from a boy who wouldn't hesitate to bulldog a steer or break a wild mustang.

"Ma'am," he said, turning to meet her eyes again, "I know I'm just a hired hand, but would it be all right if I courted Katie?" He blinked, seeming to struggle with the fact that he'd actually asked the question, then quickly added, "And if you don't mind me so much but don't like an employee courting your daughter, I could quit the ranch and find other work here-abouts if that would make it okay, you know, for me to come a calling."

Nora lifted her chin a little, letting just the hint of a smile play across her features. "Well, Lonnie, I certainly appreciate the straightforward way you're handling this. Straightforward-ness is a quality I appreciate in Mr. Bullard, who will, of course, want to weigh in on this matter before I give you an answer."

Lonnie dipped his head. "Yes, ma'am. Come to think of it, I should've waited to talk to both of y'all. I didn't mean no disre-spect to Mr. Bullard, and I sure didn't mean to put you in a fix, ma'am. I just really wanted to ask is all."

"No need to apologize, Lonnie. As I said, I do appreciate you speaking so directly. When my husband comes home, I will find the right time to speak to him on your behalf."

"Thank you, ma'am. I sure do appreciate it."

When they reached Dos Pesos, Lonnie volunteered to take care of the buggy and asked Nora how he could help her.

"Thank you for asking, Lonnie. I might pick up a few things at Mueller's before we leave, but for now, I'm going to go meet with our builder. You go on ahead and do whatever you need to do, and I'll find you when I'm finished."

"All right, ma'am, if you're certain. I'm heading to the mercantile on business of my own, though. You sure I can't pick something up for you while I'm there?"

"No, thank you, Lonnie. Until I settle matters with Mr. Zimmerman, I'll be too preoccupied to think about flour and sugar."

"Yes, ma'am."

They parted and she paused there for a second, watching the tall, young man walk off toward Mueller's with his empty saddle bags draped over one shoulder.

She wondered why he brought the saddlebag and what he meant to fill it with. It was none of her business, of course, but she couldn't help wondering.

She'd never seen Lonnie use tobacco.

Could he be buying jerky? Candy?

Neither of those items would require saddlebags.

Maybe he intended to fill the bags with airtights, his own personal supply of peaches or something like that.

Could be.

Or maybe he had an entrepreneurial streak and was filling

the bags with tobacco after all, intending to sell it to the other hands for a profit.

Or perhaps he was just picking things up for the other men out of kindness.

Whatever the case, Lonnie seemed like a nice boy. And she really did appreciate his directness. She hoped Justice would, too.

But she wouldn't hold her breath. For one reason or another, Justice didn't trust the boy. She figured that had very little to do with Lonnie, however, and a whole lot to do with the fact that a boy, any boy, was interested in Justice's little girl.

She crossed the street, excitement building in her as she approached the office of Mr. Zimmerman.

Justice had telegraphed from Fredericksburg that morning, letting her know that all was well and that her mother had spoken of starting to spend her winters in New Mexico.

The closing words of the telegraph had made her heart sing. They had also been pure Justice.

Let's build her a house (stop) Talk to Mr. Zimmerman when you're in town (stop) Love and miss you (stop) Justice.

So it was with great excitement that she walked into the office of Mr. Zimmerman and told him that yes, she was back again, and they already wanted him to build another house.

Mr. Zimmerman was pleased. And no surprise there. They always paid on time and treated him and his men well.

He believed they could begin work in around five or six weeks.

Bursting with happiness, Nora paid Zimmerman a four-hundred-dollar deposit and said goodbye, and the builder thanked her and got up and shook her hand and held the door for her to leave.

How she loved Justice at that moment. They were building a house for Mother!

But then she stepped out into the street and heard the shouting and forgot all about the new house.

"Not one more minute!" Rosa shouted with obvious rage as she stormed out of the Dos Pesos Inn, followed closely by its red-faced owner, Mervin Packer. "Not one more second!"

Packer smiled uncomfortably, noticing the folks who'd stopped to stare. "Rosa, please, can't we go back inside and talk?" He chuckled nervously, his face redder even than Rosa's hot sauce. "No need to get hysterical."

"Hysterical?" Rosa shouted. "How dare you? I am a Godly woman, Mr. Packer, and I am through fending off your filthy advances!"

The gathering crowd responded with a mixed chorus of gasps and laughter.

Nora merely smiled as the deeply offended cook took off her apron and threw it into her employer's face.

God certainly worked in mysterious ways.

CHAPTER 31

"See, I just think maybe you gotta have a little more faith in Katie is all I'm saying," Matt said as they approached the White Elephant Saloon.

They'd tied up the horses a couple doors down, well out of the way of any lead that was fixing to fly. Justice figured they'd best take care of business quickly, though. Horses that fine wouldn't last long in a town as wild as Fort Worth.

"I hear you, little brother. It's not Katie I'm worried about. It's that longhaired cowboy."

"Don't even bother going in there," said a heavyset prostitute that came pushing through the batwings.

Behind her the saloon was curiously quiet for this time of night. No music, no laughter, just a handful of loud voices echoing strangely in a room meant for more people.

"Why's that, ma'am?" Justice asked.

"They's some men in there, four of them, real rough and rowdy types, making trouble for anybody walks in. Most everybody left. I ain't even seen Pete, he's the bartender, for half an hour. I was sitting on this rough one's laps, and he was saying what they was fixing to do to me? Horrible stuff, things like I ain't never heard. Well, let me tell you, I was scared half to death, but I just kept on smiling and acting dumb, and finally I told 'em I had to go to the little girls' room, but let me tell you, I wouldn't go back in there for love nor money, no sir, and if you got half a brain, you won't go in there, neither."

Matt turned to Justice. "I never was too bright. You?"

Justice shook his head. "Sadly, no. You ready?"

"Hold on," the woman said. "Didn't you two hear a word I just said? Those men are drunk as skunks and their fixing to kill somebody."

"Well, that doesn't sound very nice," Matt said. "Maybe we should go in there and teach those men some manners."

Justice nodded. "Sounds like they could use a lesson."

The woman looked back and forth between them and tilted her head a little. "You two lawmen?"

"Nah," Matt said. "Is there a lawman in town to handle this for us?"

The woman snorted. "Sheriff Pratt was the first one to walk out when they came walking in. You boys is on your own."

"Oh well," Matt said, hitching his gun belt for show. "We never were very lucky that way, were we, big brother?"

Justice shook his head. "Nope. But at least handling trouble yourself builds character."

"That it does," Matt said. "That it does."

"We thank you for the warning and your concern, ma'am," Justice said, and handed the woman a silver dollar.

"Well, thank you, mister," she said and hurried off before they could haul her into a mix-up.

They pushed through the batwings and spread apart, Matt going left, Justice going right.

The saloon was empty, save for a couple of old drunks at the bar and four men sitting at the opposite end of the establishment, talking loudly and pounding whiskey. Within the heavy blue haze of tobacco smoke hanging over their table, revolvers sat like .45 caliber collateral atop the chips and cards covering the table.

One of the men—Clay Benner, Justice registered, matching the man's face with the wanted poster folded in his back pocket —had his back to the wall. Benner saw them coming and said something to the others, who stopped laughing and reached unhurriedly for their shooting irons.

"What do you want?" One of them—Hamilton, Justice realized—called out in a tone of surly drunkenness.

Justice's eyes flicked to the remaining two men and pegged them instantly as the other two gang members.

"We thought maybe you boys might want to play cards," Matt said with a grin.

"Heh. Cards?" Plug Morton said, scratching his patchy beard with the muzzle of his big dragoon. "Siddown, and we'll skin all y'all alive."

"No can do, partner," Matt said. "See we were thinking of playing cards, but then we remembered."

"Remembered what?" Benner growled.

"Remembered we don't play cards with a bunch of back-shooting cowards," Justice said.

A second later, everything was shouting and gunfire, the

concussion of big pistols stealing the air from the room as everyone opened fire at once.

Justice's 8-gauge roared, filling the space.

Two of the killers dropped, coming apart before they hit the floor, and another slammed against the wall, plugged by Matt's bullet.

Benner hollered and overturned the table, but Justice blew a hole through it with his remaining barrel.

Matt emptied his Colt, poking holes here and there in the table.

Benner cried out and did not return fire.

Justice reloaded.

Matt holstered one Colt and pulled the other.

Then they approached carefully from opposite sides.

Caution is always warranted in moments like these, of course, but once they saw what remained of Benner behind that perforated table, they quickly understood that he would never pose them or anybody trouble ever again.

They confirmed that the others were dead, too. Then, as Justice rooted through the dead killers' pockets, Matt reloaded the Colt he'd emptied.

"This kid, Lonnie, he just doesn't sound that bad to me," Matt said. "I mean, other than that he's a boy and he likes Katie. Why don't you just reserve judgment until you hear what Nora has to say? I'm sure she's been watching them like a hawk. Maybe he's harmless. And young girls are fickle as the wind. Maybe, you give the kid a chance, Katie'll change her mind the next day and tell him to take a hike. That sure would be better than you giving him both barrels."

Justice nodded, pocketing a fat roll of bills he'd found inside Plug Morton's boot. "Yeah, maybe you're right, little brother."

"What was that?"

"Maybe you're right."

"I heard you. I just didn't believe a man so stubborn as you could actually utter the words. Say 'em again."

"You do know I reloaded my scattergun, don't you?"

"All right, all right," Matt laughed. "Hey, I call dibs on that pearl-handled Bowie over there."

CHAPTER 32

Sitting on the porch, Katie watched with great warmth as Lonnie stammered through the final line, blushing, as he often did when he read aloud.

"Lonnie!" she exclaimed. "That was wonderful! You are learning so quickly."

Grinning, he turned a deeper shade of red.

She thought it was very endearing, especially in such a strong man.

"Aw, shucks, Katie. Thanks. But I sure don't feel wonderful. I sound dumber than a fence post."

"Three weeks ago, you didn't know the alphabet, Lonnie. Now, you're reading aloud. It's simply amazing how quickly you're learning." She stared into his eyes. "Don't get frustrated, please. Just stay patient, and you'll get it, okay? It will be worth the wait, I promise."

He held her gaze for a second. "Don't worry, Katie. I don't

have any quit in me. I set my sights on something, I'm patient as a drunken toad."

She laughed. "I love the way you talk. You say such funny things."

"Well, thanks, but I got something serious I want to say to you now, Katie," he said, handing her the primer and reaching down to open the saddle bag he'd brought to his nightly lesson. "I got you a little something."

"You did?" She was surprised and thrilled.

"I just wanted to say thanks for helping me. For teaching me to read, I mean. So I got you this."

Lonnie handed her a rectangular present wrapped clumsily in newspaper. She knew at once that it was a book and smiled. "You got me a book?"

He nodded. "Go ahead now, open it up. I hope you like it."

Feeling a little surge of excitement, Katie peeled away the newspaper and gasped.

"*Great Expectations!* I love this book!"

Lonnie beamed. "I'm so glad. After you mentioned it, I went to the store. That was the day of the cowboy contest. I meant to give it to you then, but they didn't have a copy, so I had to special order it."

"Thank you, Lonnie," Katie said, blinking away tears. "That is the sweetest thing anyone has ever done for me. But why did you do it?"

"I wanted to thank you for teaching me."

"Seeing you progress so quickly is already a gift to me, but thank you, Lonnie. Thank you so much." She clutched the book to her chest, loving the heavy solidity of it. "I absolutely love it."

"Seeing your smile makes it worth every penny and then some. There's something else, Katie. On the ride into town…"

He stopped, blushing deeply.

"What is it, Lonnie?"

He laughed and shook his head. "I don't think twice climbing on a bronc or facing bandits or rounding up long-horns in a thicket, but here I am with something to say, and I'm shaking like a pup in a thunderstorm." He held out his trembling hand to demonstrate.

"It's okay, Lonnie. Just go ahead. You can say anything to me. Anything at all."

He took a deep breath and let it out. "Well, pardon me if I'm chasing mirages here, but on the ride into town with your mama, I told her I'd like to…"

When he paused again, Katie leaned forward slightly. Her mouth was dry, and her heart was pounding in her chest. She felt like she was standing at the edge of a high cliff. "Yes?"

"I asked her permission to… court you."

With his words, Katie leapt off the cliff, but instead of falling into the void, she soared like an eagle borne upon warm drafts of pure bliss. "Oh Lonnie, that makes me so happy!"

He offered a hopeful smile. "It does?"

She wiped at fresh tears, feeling foolish, and nodded. "Yes," she laughed. "So very happy. What did Mama say?"

Lonnie shrugged. "She didn't seem opposed to the notion, but she said to ask your daddy, and then I kicked myself for not waiting on him. I don't want to come across like I was sneaking around behind his back, you know? I guess I just wanted to ask so bad I didn't think it through was all."

"I'm so glad you asked, Lonnie, and I'm so glad you told me."

Impulsively, she reached out and gave his hand a squeeze. It was big and strong and hard from work. She thrilled at the feel of it, at its size and hardness.

Then she pulled her hand back, not wanting Mama or anyone to see.

Realizing what she'd done, touching his hand like that, her face burned, and she knew she was blushing deep red.

Lonnie looked down at his hand as if he could see her fingerprints there. Then he smiled, looked at her face, and laughed nervously.

"If your pa says it's okay for me to court you, I sure would like to hold your hand sometime, Katie."

Katie's heart fluttered. "I'd like that, too. Very much. If we do start courting, what will we do?"

He laughed and shrugged again. "Honestly, I don't rightly know. I ain't never courted a girl before."

"You haven't?" she said incredulously, feeling a thrill of joy. "I figured with you being so handsome and traveling around and all, you would have had lots of girlfriends."

"Me?" He laughed. "I been too busy pushing cattle to meet girls."

"But what about when you come off the trail? I've heard stories about cowboys going to town and getting drunk and… you know."

Lonnie shook his head. "No, ma'am. Not me. Where's the honor in that? Where's the romance? Since I was just a small boy, I always knew there was one woman out there for me. Just one. And I told myself I was going to wait till I met her, no matter how long it took, and then…"

"Yes?"

"Well, what I thought was, if she liked me, too, we'd—"

Clem came around the corner then, interrupting them. He staggered over, clutching his stomach and moaning. "I think old Clem is fixin' to die, Katie girl."

"What is it, Clem?" she asked, panicked. "What's wrong? Were you poisoned?"

Clem winced and shook his head. "Asked Rosa to make some of that hot sauce and then put too much on my chili. Oh, my lands. Every time I eat her sauce, it tears me up. Feel like I swallowed a bonfire."

Realizing the one-armed hand wasn't actually dying, Katie laughed. "Why would you do that to yourself, Clem? Why don't you just skip the hot sauce?"

Clem arched one snowy eyebrow and drew his head back a little, staring at her like she was crazy. "Skip the hot sauce? Now, where would be the fun in that?"

CHAPTER 33

E xcitement built, as it always did, when Justice left the main road and rode onto the path that cut across his sprawling property.

It was good seeing Matt, and he'd unexpectedly gotten a lot out of their conversations, but he had missed home, and he'd been gone for a long time.

Off to the south of the road, he saw Pedro Martin, Silas Sutton, and Lonnie Cooper pushing the herd toward new forage.

He slowed his horse and watched them work, focusing on the golden-haired boy who had consumed so much of his thinking and talking lately.

Long hair or not, the kid could ride. Justice had to give him that. He worked like a man.

Maybe Matt's right, he thought. *Maybe the kid's okay. Maybe I have to give him a chance.*

He rode around the bend and smiled to see the ranch house.

Nora was outside, tending flowers. Seeing him, she stood and waved.

He waved back, his heart swelling with love, and rode on until a pair of shaggy furballs raced from the brush to growl and snap at the bay's heels.

The bay was a good horse, solid in a gunfight, but he was no Dagger or Bourbon. Panicked by the pups' ambush, he set to bucking and kicking.

"Hey!" Justice shouted and held on for dear life as the horse broke and ran, followed by the miniature wolves.

It was a good fifty feet before Justice got the horse calmed down again. He looked back, ready to holler at the pups, but saw they had been intercepted by a growling Rafer, who had them on their backs.

I gotta work on those pups, Justice thought, marveling at how much they'd grown in his absence, *or somebody's gonna get thrown from a horse.*

He rode the rest of the way.

Smiling up at him, Nora wiped the back of her hand across her perspiring forehead, leaving a streak of dirt across one brow.

Standing there, looking so much like herself and now showing even more, she had never looked so beautiful to him.

"Welcome home, Mr. Bullard."

"Thank you, Mrs. Bullard. I sure am happy to set eyes on you."

He got down and hugged and kissed her, and she walked with him into the stable, and they talked as he cared for the bay.

She asked about his trip, and he told her how it had gone.

At some point, Rafer came trotting in, followed by the

shaggy, flop-eared pups, who glanced at him with uncharacteristic sheepishness, reminding him of kids feeling jumpy after
getting the switch.

"Where's Eli?"

"Picking peppers for dinner."

"And Katie?"

Nora smiled. "She's cooking with Rosa."

"Rosa? You mean to tell me Katie took a job at the Dos Pesos
Inn?"

Nora shook her head, smiling more broadly. "Remember
what I said about staying out of God's way? Well, I did, and He
answered my prayers. Last time I was in town, Rosa came
storming out of the inn the very moment I was walking past."

"She quit?"

"She did."

Justice pushed his hat back, glanced at the newly finished
guesthouse, and ran his tongue around the inside of his cheek
in a slow circle. "Well now, if Rosa's the new cook, I might have
to give up being a silent justice and sign on as a hand for this
ranch."

Nora laughed. "Are you complaining about the old cook?"

"No, ma'am. Certainly not. The old cook is wonderful. But
that doesn't mean I can't also like Rosa's grub."

Nora crossed her arms. "Mhmm. Well, if you treat Rosa
right, she might let you snitch some of her chili."

"Now you're talking my language, Mrs. Bullard. Let's go on
over to the guesthouse. I'll welcome Rosa and get a hug from
my little girl. I missed seeing her sitting around with her nose
jammed in a book."

"That's not all Katie's interested in these days."

"I know." He was surprised to feel a surge of protectiveness bordering on anger. Hadn't he and Matt hashed out the situation?

Well, maybe hashing out a situation and stepping back into it were two different things, he reckoned. He'd just have to give it time and hold his tongue until he felt better about things.

A man who couldn't control his emotions was doomed to a life of suffering.

Besides, now wasn't the time to go sour over Katie's interest in Lonnie. It was time for a happy reunion, and he couldn't wait to see her reaction when she saw what he'd brought her from Fredericksburg.

Justice retrieved his saddlebags, and they walked over to the guesthouse. He admired the finished touches as he crossed the porch and went inside.

"Pa!" Katie cried and ran from the kitchen into his arms.

"Hello, little girl. I sure did miss you."

"I missed you, too, Pa! Welcome home."

For a few seconds, he just held her, wishing the moment could go on forever.

Then a smiling Rosa emerged from the kitchen, accompanied by a cloud of wonderful aromas. "Welcome home, Mr. Bullard."

"Rosa, it's great to see you, and please call me Justice. I was happy to hear you'd joined us. Are you settling in all right? Do you need anything?"

Rosa said she was settling in well and didn't need anything but promised to let them know if that changed.

When Rosa drifted back into the kitchen, Justice told Katie, "I brought you a little something from Fredericksburg, sweetie."

He held up the saddlebag and rapped the side, letting her hear the tell-tale *thunk-thunk* of knuckles on a hardcover.

"Another book?" Nora said, smiling. "You are going to spoil her, Justice."

Katie's eyes lit up. She was a girl who asked for little and appreciated everything, but nothing made her happier than receiving a new book.

Justice pulled out the book, happy that Emma had wrapped it in paper for him. "Here you go, Katie. I have a sneaking suspicion you're gonna like this one."

"Thanks, Pa! I can't wait to see what it is." Katie worked at the brown paper and pulled it neatly apart, shucking the book.

Justice grinned, waiting for the squeal of elation once she saw what he'd tracked down for her.

But seeing the cover, Katie sort of froze. Then her smile dimmed a touch. "Oh, Pa. Thank you. I do love *Great Expectations* so much."

He nodded. "I figured you did since you've borrowed Mr. Mueller's copy… how many times is it now, three?"

"Four. And yes, it's my favorite book. Thank you. Really."

He tilted his head a little. "But…"

Katie offered a timid smile. "But I already have a copy."

Now, he was really confused. "How? Mr. Mueller never carried it."

"No, but Lonnie asked Mr. Mueller to special order a copy for me. It was the day Lonnie won the cowboy contest. He went straight to the mercantile and spent some of his winnings to buy me *Great Expectations*. Wasn't that nice of him? Isn't that just the sweetest thing?"

CHAPTER 34

L ater, when Nora offered to prepare a bath for him, Justice shook his head. "Not going to happen, my love."

Nora smirked. "Hmm. How do I put this diplomatically? After summer travel between Texas and New Mexico Territory, you are smelling slightly less than fresh, dear husband."

He laughed, petting Tilly, the skinny cat he'd brought home from Texas. "That was diplomatic enough. Like an iron fist in a velvet glove. Look, I know I stink, and I'm fixing to take care of it. But I won't have my pregnant wife lugging water for me."

"I can manage."

"I know you can, but why bother when I can just jump in the river and scrub up?"

"Are you sure? Wouldn't a nice bath be relaxing?"

"I don't want to relax, I want to get clean. Besides, it'll give me a chance to take Dagger. I'm sure he's chomping at the bit. There's a horse that likes to ride."

"He does, which is why I've been having Lonnie ride him some each day."

Justice's hackles rose. "Lonnie's been riding Dagger?"

Nora nodded. "You always liked it when I had Silas or Pedro ride him, so I figured—"

"It's all right. You did the right thing. It's just that Lonnie's name keeps popping up is all."

"I'm sorry about the mix up with the books."

"Ah, that's nothing. If she keeps the copy I got her nice, maybe she could swap it for a different book at Mueller's."

"I think probably she could. But I know you were disappointed. You sure you don't want a nice, warm bath?"

"I'm sure. Now, if you will excuse me, Mrs. Bullard, I'm gonna go wash the stink off before my wife objects."

He fetched a change of clothes, a bar of soap, and a towel, threw it all in a haversack, and went out, got Dagger, and rode south along the river, getting far enough from the cattle crossing to avoid picking up leeches.

The day was hot, but the river was merely warm, fed by mountain streams as it was.

It felt good to get cleaned up. He toweled off, put on clean clothes, and stuffed his sweaty trail duds into the haversack.

Ground hitched on the bank, Dagger foraged contentedly.

"What do you say, partner? You ready to ride back?"

The horse blinked at him then lifted his head, ears twitching.

A second later, Justice heard the sound of approaching hooves.

Out of long habit, he unfastened his hammer loops.

And Lonnie Cooper rode into view atop his mahogany bay stallion.

Spotting Justice, the boy nodded. "Sir."

"What is it, Lonnie?"

"Mind if I climb down?"

"Come on down. Everything all right?"

"Yes, sir," Lonnie said, dismounting and dropping the stallion's reins. "I just been wanting to talk to you about something is all."

Why did the boy look so nervous?

"Go ahead. Talk."

The boy examined the ground for a second then lifted his chin and looked Justice in the eyes, his gaze full of determination. "Sir, I'm sweet on your daughter."

Justice gritted his teeth. He hadn't expected this. His mind took a step back. "Katie?"

"Yes, sir. She's the nicest person I ever done met, and she's teaching me to read, and well, sir, I'd like to ask your permission to court her."

Justice blinked at him.

He could see the kid was nervous, but Lonnie stood his ground, not breaking eye contact.

He had sand, anyway.

"You want to court Katie."

"Yes, sir. I know I'm just a cowboy, but—"

"She's only sixteen."

"Yes, sir. I'm ten months her senior. Almost ten months."

What Justice wanted to do in that moment was pick the kid up and throw him in the river. But instead, he harkened back to his conversations with Matt.

Lonnie waited in silence, not so much squirming as looking like he wanted to squirm.

Justice understood how he felt. This had rattled his own cage.

"Just what is your notion of courting, Lonnie?"

"I don't rightly know, sir. To tell you the truth, I ain't never courted a girl before."

"No?"

"No, sir."

Staring at the kid, remembering him coming out of the mercantile and how stupid he had looked, sucking on the hard candy with his long hair, he found himself believing Lonnie.

"Well, then, let me tell you what courting means to me."

Lonnie waited.

"What courting means is talking," Justice explained, wishing he could just leave it at that, "and maybe taking walks together."

Now, the kid was fighting a grin. "Yes, sir."

"Walks chaperoned by Mrs. Bullard or me, that is."

"Yes, sir. Of course, sir."

"Of course? I thought you didn't know anything about courting."

"I don't, sir. All I know is I think the world of Katie and being able to walk with her and talk with her sounds mighty fine."

"Well, don't get too excited. I haven't said okay yet, have I?"

"No, sir."

"And for all I know, Katie might say no."

"She might, sir."

"But you doubt it."

"Honestly, I do, sir. Her and me enjoy one another's company."

"Well, you just make sure you don't go enjoying each other's company too much, you got me?"

"Yes, sir. You can trust me. I will be nothing but respectful if you allow me to court her."

Justice studied him for a few silent seconds, looking for something—he wasn't sure what—and not finding it.

"All right, Lonnie. You have my permission. But if you overstep your boundaries, you and me are gonna have a problem. You understand?"

"I understand, sir. I won't do like you said and overstep anything. You have my word, sir."

With that, the boy stuck out his hand.

Justice looked at it for a second, then shook. The kid's hand was damp with sweat, but his grip was firm and calloused, and he looked Justice in the eye.

Could be worse, Justice thought. In fact, if Lonnie wasn't after Katie, he might even like the kid.

"All right. Get out of here and get back to work before I dock your pay. I'll go talk to Katie and Mrs. Bullard. Tonight after supper, you come on over to the house, and the two of you can sit on the porch and talk for a spell."

"Yes, sir," Lonnie said, a big smile breaking across his face. "Thank you, sir."

CHAPTER 35

The next several days were strange ones for Justice. It was great to be home, of course, and he was never happier than he was with his family.

But he was uncharacteristically tense, and by the end of each night, his neck and shoulders felt like he'd spent the day digging ditches.

Lonnie, who proved to be top hand as reported, appeared to be minding his manners with Katie, but every burst of laughter from the porch set Justice's teeth on edge.

As if that wasn't enough, somebody—usually Katie or Eli—was always mentioning the cowboy's name.

Even he and Nora mentioned Lonnie during their nightly talks.

"Try to give them a little space, Justice," Nora advised one night as they were getting ready to bed down.

"Space? I give them space."

"You lurk near the window."

"I don't trust him."

"He's a nice boy."

"He's a boy. That's all that needs saying. You give a boy space with a girl, it's only a matter of time until he—"

"I think he's being sincere, Justice."

"That's what I'm worried about. Am I the only one who remembers how young she is?"

"Many women marry younger than sixteen."

"Many women, maybe, but not my daughter. Besides, she's different. She had a different kind of childhood, losing her folks and coming up in the orphanage. She's still very childlike in many ways."

"To you, perhaps, but she's changing, Justice, becoming a young woman. What do you want her to do, stay a child forever?"

"No, you know I don't."

"I know, but still."

"I just don't want her to do anything stupid."

"So says every parent in history."

"Every loving parent, anyway."

"Yes, and you are a loving parent, Justice. Katie's very lucky to have you. As is Eli." She placed a hand on her distended belly and smiled. "So is this little one."

"Not half so lucky as they are to have you as their mama," Justice said, and leaned down to kiss her tummy.

He stayed busy working around the place and visiting neighboring ranches.

Diego chuckled when Justice told him of the puppies, who had continued to grow at an unsettling rate and who still stalked him every time he crossed open ground, even though they had learned not to attack him. With Eli, they would still jump on him from behind, knock him to the ground, and finish him with licking.

"The females take after their mother," Diego said. "I believe they might make cattle dogs. But speaking of females, any suitors sniffing around yet?"

"Funny you should mention that," Justice said, and filled him in.

Diego grinned. "You want me to shoot him?"

"Not yet."

Justice also visited the Lopezes, who told him they were thinking of selling their ranch. Roberto could get around with a cane now, but the family had never really healed from Tucker's attack on their home, not in their hearts and minds, where healing matters most.

They had followed Justice's advice and hired some hands, but Justice sensed they weren't comfortable having others do their work. Some folks just aren't cut out for hiring employees.

"Well," he told them, "if you leave, you'll be missed, but hey, if you do decide to sell, let me know, all right? Your property abuts mine. I'd give you a good price, more than fair. Not that I'm encouraging you to sell. You're good neighbors."

He meant what he said but had to admit he'd like to own the property. If he bought the Lopez ranch, his land would stretch all the way down to the cattleman association's open range and clubhouse.

The Lopezes thanked him, and he headed home, where there was always plenty to do.

He needed to go to town and check to make sure the Texas

bounties had arrived in his bank account, but he kept finding reasons not to leave home.

Mostly, that was because he loved being with his family.

But also, there was the matter that had been keeping his shoulders all bunched up.

Some part of his mind, no matter how ridiculous it was, felt like the moment he left, the moment he took his eyes off Katie and Lonnie, they were gonna do a lot more than just talk.

Then, one day when he was shoeing the strawberry roan, Eli came running into the stable, chased by his multicolored shadows.

Rafer lifted his head and stared at the trio.

"Pa!" Eli gasped, breathing hard.

Justice let go of the horse's freshly shod hoof. "What is it, son? What's wrong?"

"It's Katie," Eli huffed.

"What is it? What's wrong?"

"And Lonnie," Eli puffed.

"What is it?" Justice said, his blood running cold. "What's wrong with them?"

"They was smooching!"

"Smooching?" Justice got to his feet. He blinked at Eli while his mind whirled. For as surprised as he was, another part of his mind nodded nastily, having known all along that this moment would come. "Are you certain?"

"Well, not dead certain, Pa, but it looked like they was smooching."

"Where?"

"On the lips, I reckon. I couldn't really see their faces. Just, they was hugging and all, so—"

"I mean, where are they?"

"Over behind the bunkhouse."

Behind the bunkhouse? His mind raced. What was Katie doing behind the bunkhouse?

His five-pointed scar did not burn, but the rest of him burst into white-hot anger. He glanced at his hand and realized he was holding the same farrier hammer he'd used to kill Tate back when all this started.

He dropped the hammer to the stable floor, balled his big hands into fists, and marched toward the bunkhouse, ready to knot a golden scalp to his belt.

He heard them before he saw them.

Heard Katie's laughter, then her voice. "I've been wanting to do this for so long, Lonnie. You have no idea."

"Me, too, Katie, but I don't think—"

Justice came around the corner, ready to kill.

Lonnie had Katie by the shoulders, as if holding her at arm's length. Spotting Justice, he dropped his hands. His eyes went wide, and all the color drained from his face.

Following Lonnie's gaze, Katie saw Justice and gave a terrified little yelp. "Pa!"

"Get in the house, Katie," Justice growled. "Now."

"But Pa, I can explain. It was my fault. I—"

"In the house. Now."

"Yes, Pa." And the girl hurried away around the corner.

"You," Justice said, marching toward Lonnie, who held up his palms defensively.

"I'm sorry, Mr. Bullard. We were just—"

"I trusted you to respect her."

"I do respect Katie," Lonnie said, standing his ground. "And I love her."

"Love her?"

"Yes, sir. I love her."

"You broke your promise."

"I didn't mean to—"

"You broke your promise. The courtship's off."

"Please don't say that, sir. I love her."

"Not anymore, you don't. I won't have you corrupting my daughter. If you want to keep your job, you're gonna have to forget all about Katie."

"I could never."

"Well, then you'd best pack your bags. Because no hand of mine is going to go smooching my daughter."

"We wasn't smooching, sir. We was just—"

"What's your choice, Lonnie? Stick around and steer clear of Katie, or go find another job?"

Lonnie stared back at him, his eyes once again filled with determination. His voice, on the other hand, sounded very sad. "Well, then, sir, if those are my choices, I reckon I'd best get hunting new work. Because there ain't no way I will ever forget Katie. I will always love her."

"All right, then. Pack up and hit the road."

CHAPTER 36

A few days later, when Doc's telegram arrived, Justice received it with mixed emotions.

Lonnie was gone.

Katie was heartbroken.

That first day, she'd sobbed and sobbed, insisting it was all her fault, insisting that all they'd done was hug, insisting that Lonnie hadn't even wanted to do that, that she'd gone hunting him and embraced him just before Eli came running around the corner.

Justice suspected she was telling the truth. Her little brother had probably imagined the smooching part.

But what did that change?

Even if Lonnie hadn't broken his promise, Katie's lack of control showed how dangerous it was for the two of them to live on the same ranch.

No, he'd made the right decision. He was sure of it.

But the notion that Lonnie might be innocent, that the boy

had kept his promise yet still ended up losing his job did bother Justice.

But what could he do?

Nothing, that was what.

It was like his dilemma on the trail.

You could never set everything right. Not really.

You just had to do your best and keep moving. If you made mistakes, learn from them. But dwelling on imperfection is a fool's errand… especially when perfection isn't possible.

And with Katie's situation, there could be no perfection.

She remained her dutiful self. She did her chores and helped Rosa cook for the men and sat with Eli, listening as he read his primer, but she was a ghost of her former self, sad and slouching and quiet.

He sure did wish she would smile again.

Nora told him to be patient, that Katie was indeed heart-broken but would come back to them in time.

He hadn't talked to Katie about things since sitting her down the day it all happened. He wouldn't know what to say, and he didn't want to make her cry again.

He'd sooner face half a dozen bad men with Winchesters than try to talk to a teenage girl about her feelings.

Which was why, when Doc's orders arrived, Justice felt a degree of relief. The telegram meant escaping long, confounding days full of stillness and sorrow and returning to the trail, where he could get back to killing bad men and helping folks in need.

But at the same time, he was a man who hoed his own rows. He always took care of his horses before seeing to himself, always took care of his gear, always kept his weapons clean and ready. And always, always, always did the best he could for his family.

So he hated to leave the ranch without patching up things with Katie and loathed the relief he felt as he might a kind of fledgling cowardice.

"Just give it time," Nora told him again, as he saddled Dagger. "You go save lives, and I'll take care of Katie."

She was right, of course, so as Justice set off, he did his best to push Katie's sorrow and all questions of Lonnie from his mind.

His line of work demanded complete focus. Anything less could get you killed.

And he wasn't setting out against just anybody.

Cyrus Undergrove and his murderous gang had ridden back across the border.

They'd been seen heading northwest, leaving Texas, and slipping into New Mexico Territory.

Given their trajectory, Doc figured they might be heading for Albuquerque or Bernalillo. Or they might angle northwest and hit Santa Fe. It was impossible to say.

So Doc wanted Justice to ride south on a general sweep, dispensing justice as usual but keeping his eyes and ears open and reporting any news to Doc, who could mobilize law enforcement if they got a bead on the gang.

After a day's ride, Justice ground hitched Dagger to forage by the river, and cooked up a dinner of beans and pork belly, which he enjoyed with some of the bread Rosa had packed and a pot of steaming coffee.

He studied the papers on the Undergrove Gang as he ate.

That night, he had trouble falling asleep. He lay in his bedroll, staring up at the stars, trying not to think about Katie.

It didn't work.

Finally, he said a prayer. "Lord, I'm pretty good at killing wicked men, but I don't know much about girls. Please help Katie feel better."

He blinked up at the sky a few times, knowing there was more to say, and added, "And Lord, if I made a mistake, please show me, and please help me to know how to fix things."

The prayer surprised him. He wasn't one to second-guess himself.

Nora often said the Holy Spirit helps us to pray correctly when we can't find the way ourselves. Was that what had just happened?

Whatever the case, after the prayer, he finally slipped off to sleep.

He got an early start the next morning. The day was hot and dry, and he stopped frequently to let Dagger drink from the river.

Around noon, he came to a small ranch, where a solitary old man leaned on a crutch, struggling to mend a broken fence.

He was a big man with broad shoulders and bright white hair. He strained, sweating profusely, trying to manage a sledgehammer with one hand. His grip was choked way up close to the head, and he growled miserably, pounding awkwardly on a half-buried post while trying to balance on the crutch, his left leg gimped up like that of a limping hound packing an injured paw.

Hearing Justice, he looked up. Sweat glistened on his red

face. "I feel like a one-legged cat trying to bury a turd on a frozen lake."

Justice chuckled. "Mind if I climb down and give you a hand?"

"I'd be much obliged," the man said. "My name's Prima, Abner Prima."

Justice shook his hand. It was big and calloused and slick with sweat.

"Glad I happened to be passing through. My name's Justice Bullard."

"Justice, huh? And just when I'd started to think there wasn't no justice left in the world."

"I'm still here," Justice said. "Let's mend this fence."

CHAPTER 37

After a couple of hours, they broke for dinner.

"The maid run off with the butler," Prima joked as they went inside the unkempt kitchen. "How many eggs you want?"

"One'll do."

"Working the way you work? I got plenty. How many can you eat."

"One'll fix me up just fine. It's hot."

"That it is. Well, I sure am glad you came along when you did. Now that I got that fence fixed, all I gotta do is clean up the waterhole and drive the cows over. They've grazed the back pasture to stubble."

"What are you running?"

"Just a small herd. A dozen cows, a few steers, and one mean bull. Longhorns. Lately, folks around here been moving to angus. They bulk up, get you more at market, but I'll stick with my longhorns. They'll keep at that stubble until I get this pasture fixed up. Longhorns'll live on forage that'd kill other breeds. I got a feeling half of them big angus'll die out first real drought we get."

"Well, no need for your cattle to eat sand. I'll help you get that waterhole mucked out."

Prima plated the fried eggs. "I'd be mighty thankful. I could pay a dollar a day for as long as you could stay on. I got two weeks of work. Probably even three or four if you ain't got plans elsewhere."

"I do."

Prima nodded, looking disappointed. He pushed aside dirty dishes, making two places at the table, and set down the plates. "Well, you help me with that water hole, I'll pay you a dollar today. Here, eat up."

Justice sat down, bowed his head in silent prayer, and went to work on the egg. "Thanks for the offer, but I don't want any money. I got everything I need, and I'm happy to lend a hand."

"I'd appreciate that. I truly would. Sure you don't want any money?"

"Positive."

"Well, at least let me feed you and give you a place to lay your head."

"All right."

Prima looked around at the mess, blinking, likely trying to imagine how Justice was seeing it. "Truth be told, the place has fallen into disrepair since my leg got hurt. The more I sit, the more I feel like sitting. Some days, it's all I can do just to get out of bed and feed myself. It ain't just my leg. It's my heart."

"You look healthy enough except for the leg."

"My heart's healthy enough. It's just broke is all."

"Woman trouble?"

"In a manner of speaking. My wife died a year back. She's buried on the side of the house."

"My condolences. I noticed the cross."

"She was a good woman, old Mattie. Put up with my nonsense all those years and raised a fine young daughter."

He paused, his eyes going momentarily out of focus. "I miss my daughter." He sighed. "Feel like my heart's been torn out. It's my own fault she's gone. I never was good at talking with her. But we got along real good. Then Mother died, and well, we were both hurting, and I was quiet all the time, and Jessie met this young fella, and I wasn't too happy about it."

Prima shook his head and wiped his dirty shirt sleeve at the corners of his glistening eyes. "Ain't I mess?" he laughed.

"You're all right."

Prima shook his head. "Nope. I am not. Not since Jessie ran off with her beau. I was a fool, trying to keep them apart, then blowing up the way I did. I forced her to choose. And what's a young girl full of life gonna choose? This?" He spread his hands and twisted, indicating the dirty house. "Or life in town with a young fella who loves her? I reckon they're married now, and I further reckon I ain't even welcome at their home."

"Well, you won't know until you try. Sometimes, I reckon we get a notion that things are worse than they are, especially with women. Sometimes, women just need a little time is all."

Prima shook his head. "I was so desperate to hold onto her that I drove her off. Now, look at me. All alone with a bad leg."

"You need a doctor?"

Prima shrugged. "I don't heal like I used to. But I'll tell you the truth. You could lop off my leg and burn this ranch to the ground if it meant I could get my Jessie back. Even with that fella in tow. Isn't that something? I don't even mind the boy all that much."

Justice leaned back, listening, his own mind wondering if maybe God was already answering his bedtime prayer.

"We men work ourselves to death for our families," Prima said. "Ain't nothing wrong with that. It's what us men are here for. We grab hold of something and keep working till the thing's done. But sometimes, we lock onto the wrong things and push too hard. Might be money, might be pride, might be our notion of how our daughters should live their lives. Sometimes, we love them so much, we drive them off."

"Ever consider going to town and telling her how you feel?"

Prima shook his head. "Can't. That's how I got this bad leg in the first place. Lucky they didn't just kill me. When you're an old man in country like this, you are vulnerable to the whims of the young."

"Somebody hurt your leg?"

Prima nodded. "The Fabers. Knocked me down, put their guns on me. Told me to lay my leg across a log, then stomped it like a snake."

Beneath Justice's sweat-soaked shirt, his five-pointed star set to burning. "Why?"

"Because they wanted to. They're mean through and through, the Fabers. Course, you ask them, they'd say it was because I didn't have enough money to the toll."

"Toll?"

"Yeah, they call it a road tax. Two or three of them set up beside the road just outside of town, stop people going in or out. Sometimes, folks get lucky and slip past when they aren't there, but if they catch you coming or going, they demand their tax."

"They kill anybody?"

"If they ain't, they will."

"Tell me more."

CHAPTER 38

K atie looked up when a smiling Eli came running into the guesthouse.

For a day or two after Pa had sent Lonnie away, she'd been angry with her little brother.

Why had Eli run and tattled on her? And why in the world had he made up the smooching stuff?

But she'd done her best not to show her anger because she loved Eli and remembered that he was just small. You learned to keep such things in mind when you grew up in an orphanage unless you wanted to live in total bitterness.

Now, her anger had passed, and seeing the boy's excited smile, she had to wonder what was happening.

It couldn't be…

But no, Lonnie respected Pa too much to come back to the ranch uninvited.

Then Eli said, "Come on out, Katie. Mueller's wagon just pulled up. We gotta help mama unload. You think maybe she ordered some candy?"

"Maybe," Katie said, following him out.

"Hey, Katie? When do you reckon you'll start smiling again?"

"I don't know, Eli. I'm pretty sad."

"It's on account of Mr. Lonnie, isn't it?"

She nodded and felt a fresh lump form in her throat. How she loved him. How she missed him. And how terribly stupid she had been.

"I'm awful sorry I said anything to Pa."

"I wish you hadn't, Eli. I really wish you hadn't."

Frowning, the boy kicked a stone. "I'm real sorry, Katie. Do you still love me?"

She hauled him into a hug, touched that a boy his age would even consider her feelings.

"Of course I still love you, Eli. Nothing could change that. And I forgive you."

She started to say, *However, please don't ever do that again*, but stopped herself, because she knew he'd never have another opportunity.

Lonnie was gone. He'd probably ridden completely out of the territory. She'd probably never even see him again. It pained her to imagine him riding off and meeting some other girl, some girl older and prettier than her with a pa who recognized Lonnie's worth.

As for her part, she would never, ever love anybody else ever again. Not the way she'd loved Lonnie.

For her, love was dead, gone the way of her poor parents.

Blinking through her tears, she saw Willie, Mr. Mueller's delivery boy, waving to her from behind the wagon.

As they drew nearer, Willie handed Eli a sack of vittles. "You strong enough to carry this inside, Eli?"

"You bet, Mr. Willie," Eli said, taking the sack with pride and heading inside the ranch house.

"Here," Willie said, handing her a square of folded paper. "Tuck that away. It's from Lonnie."

Glancing down and seeing her name scrawled across the note in blocky text, her heart leapt with joy. But as she tucked it into her dress pocket, something occurred to her.

"But Lonnie can't write."

Willie grinned and handed her a box of jars. "Paid me to write it for him. Easiest two bits I ever earned."

"Where is he?"

"Who, Lonnie? He got himself a room at Janie's."

"Janie's?"

"A boarding house in Dos Pesos. Got himself a job over at the livery, mucking out stalls and tending to the horses."

"Will you see him?"

"I see him moping around town."

She felt a pang of joy. Lonnie missed her, too! Maybe all was not actually lost.

But before she could say anything, Mama came out of the house, smiling at her. "Oh, there you are, Katie. Thank you for helping with this."

"Yes, Mama."

Later, after she'd helped unload the order, and Willie had driven off, Katie went back to the guesthouse, where Rosa was dicing onions to fry up for supper.

The black-haired woman grinned up from the cutting

board, her eyes streaming tears. "These sure are strong onions," she laughed.

Katie couldn't wait one more minute to read the note. She excused herself, went to the privy, opened the letter with trembling fingers, and read by the dim light.

DEAR KATIE,

AIN'T THIS SOME FIX WE GOT OURSELVES INTO? KATIE I LOVE YOU *sweetie and that's just what I told your pa. I got a job mucking stalls at the livery in Dos Pesos. I miss cowboying but oh well it don't matter to me because I am gonna sit right here unless you tell me you don't love me no more and then I will probably still keep setting here hoping you change your mind. Because I love you Katie and I don't care who knows that because it's true and it ain't never gonna change no matter what. You can count on that. I respect your pa so I won't never give him no trouble but I ain't never gonna give up on you Katie because I love you and that is forever and ever. I hope I can see you again sometime real soon.*

LOVE,
  Lonnie

P.S. I BOUGHT A BOOK AT THE STORE BUT IT IS TOO HARD FOR ME TO *read without your help.*

. . .

Katie clutched the letter to her bosom in the stinking confines of the privy and wept tears of joy.

Lonnie still loved her.

She could bear up under anything so long as she knew he still loved her.

But how could she be reunited with him?

CHAPTER 39

Needing supplies, Abner Prima pointed his wagon toward town.

Justice followed at a distance.

Prima rounded the corner he'd described. A second after he disappeared between two embankments, the old man's voice called, "Whoa! Whoa, mule!"

Other voices shouted, low and harsh.

With the reins in one hand and a custom Colt in the other, Justice spurred Dagger, hurried around the corner, and entered the narrow defile, where he saw a filthy pistolero standing at the center of the road, blocking the wagon.

The other two Fabers occupied opposite sides of the gulley. One was grinning like a fool and had his rifle yoked over his shoulders. The other held his rifle at belt level, pointing it vaguely in Prima's direction.

Justice shot that one first then swung the pistol in the other direction and pulled the trigger again just as the remaining rifleman took a wild shot and died for it.

The remaining Faber fired wide-eyed at Justice, fanned the hammer, fired again, then flew backward, struck in the chest by Justice's third round.

Justice whipped his head back and forth, scanning for additional threats but saw none.

"That's all they is," Prima hollered, his voice sounding high and excited and strange.

Justice nodded. The whole thing had taken three or four seconds once the lead started flying.

Prima looked at him with awe. "You sure made quick work of them, Justice."

Justice broke open the Colt and reloaded. "Never saw any percentage in dragging things out."

"I guess not. Remind me to never make you mad, all right?"

Justice snapped the gate shut again and holstered his weapon. "I don't kill out of anger. I might feel anger toward some folks I kill, but that's not why I kill them. These men had it coming."

"Yes, they did, but…" Prima trailed off, shaking his head.

"Hold steady," Justice said, getting down from Dagger, who seemed alert but unperturbed by the clash. "I'll toss them in the wagon, and we'll cart them into town and see if they have any paper on them. They got kin in town?"

"The Fabers? Sure, they got kin. But I don't reckon—"

"Anytime blood's involved," Justice said, lifting one of the men and tossing him into the back of the wagon with a thump, "you always have to reckon somebody'll come for you. I'd sooner root them out now rather than wonder if they ever came after you."

"Sounds good when you put it that way. I'm not in the habit of prying into a man's business, but what line of work are you in, anyway?"

"Like I said, I kill people who deserve it. And sometimes, in between, I help folks mend fences and muck out waterholes."

"Much obliged," Prima said, looking pale.

"I'll ride in first," Justice said. "We'll go straight to the marshal's office. Story goes we don't know each other. I'll tell the marshal I killed these highwaymen then you came along, and I told you to cart the dead for me, you hear?"

Prima nodded.

"That way, if the remaining Fabers don't give us a chance to kill them, they won't have any reason to come after you."

"All right, Justice. Whatever you say."

"And then you can go find your daughter and tell her how you feel." He started Dagger forward.

Prima sat tight.

Justice wheeled around. "You coming?"

"Truth be told, I'm starting to get cold feet."

"Why?"

"What if she hates me? What if she tells me she never wants to see me again?"

"Do you think she's gonna say those things?"

Prima shook his head and started to speak, but Justice beat him to it.

"Look, right now you're miserable. You've been living like you'd never see her again."

Prima nodded.

"So forget what you're afraid she might say. Never let fear stop you from doing what's right. Now, do you want to apologize to your daughter or not?"

Sitting up a little straighter, Prima nodded. "I used to be strong, Justice. I'm not fooling. But then—"

"Forget all that," Justice said. "Today's the day you quit looking to the past and start looking to the future. Let's go see your daughter."

As it was conceived so was it done.

They rode into town, spotted no Fabers, and dropped off their gruesome cargo with the marshal, a seemingly inept man with a small head and a large body, who took Justice's statement and walked him over to the bank, where the marshal withdrew twenty dollars to cover the bounty for all three Fabers.

Spotting the bank manager, Justice took out the wanted posters for the Undergrove Gang and warned the man they might be headed this way.

The manager was both frightened and appreciative.

Then Justice went back out to Prima. "Told them I was a bounty hunter. Now, which way to the blacksmith's shop?"

Prima led the way. They pulled up in front of the smith's shop and tethered their horses and went inside, where the air rang with the rhythmic clanging of a hammer at work. A burly man in a leather apron looked up from his anvil with a startled expression, then stepped cautiously forward, the hammer still in hand.

"Is Jessie here?" Prima asked.

"Why?" the young blacksmith, apparently Jessie's husband,

asked. "She's happy now, Mr. Prima. And you should know we're married. I won't have you coming in here and shouting at her."

Prima shook his head. "I won't," he said softly, his voice sounding fragile. "I just... need to see her."

The blacksmith looked at Justice. His gaze lingered on the two tied-down pistols. "You can't take her away. I'll die before I let you take Jessie from me."

"I don't want to take her away," Prima said. "I just want to see her again."

The blacksmith nodded then turned his head slightly, never taking his eyes off the pair of them, still clinging to his big hammer, as if that might offer some defense against Justice's six-shooters if it came to violence.

"Jessie," he hollered. "You'd best come on out here."

A moment later, a thin red-haired woman appeared with a look of confusion. "What is it, Charles? Is everything all—"

Her words died as she spotted her father and froze in place.

Sniffling with emotion, Prima lifted a hand and took a tentative hop forward on his crutch.

"Daddy?"

Prima nodded. "I'm so sorry, Jessie."

The young woman rushed forward and hugged her father. "Daddy, you're so thin. What happened to your leg? I've missed you so much. I wanted to visit, but I thought you would still be cross."

"No, Jessie. Never again. I'm sorry. So, so sorry."

"Oh, Daddy. Thank you for coming. I've missed you terribly!"

Justice turned on his heel and walked out, leaving them to it.

Keeping his eyes peeled for Fabers, he walked to the tele-graph station, sent Doc a quick telegram, and waited for the reply.

It didn't take long and didn't say much.

NO NEW INFORMATION (STOP) PROCEED AS PLANNED (STOP) DOC

CHAPTER 40

I n Justice's line of work, you learned to watch your back
trail.

Three miles outside of town, he topped a ridge and glassed
his backtrail and saw the three riders coming fast.

They were all tall and wiry and wore drooping slouch hats
like the Fabers.

He reckoned that's exactly what they were, but he wasn't
ready to ambush them on such thin evidence.

Scanning the trail ahead, he saw that it dipped down in a
saddle then climbed up to a still higher peak with a stony crest.

Good.

What were his options?

He thought things through for about a minute and made his
decision.

It wasn't a perfect plan, and he'd have to watch them close
with the spyglasses, but he figured it was the best course of
action.

He had considered letting Dagger bury them with speed, but you never knew when the country would open up and give pursuers a clear shot. If they had a Sharps and knew how to use it, that could mean real trouble.

With the men coming on fast, Justice didn't have much time.

Moving quickly, he rode halfway down the saddle, dismounted, pulled out the affidavit he'd gotten for turning over the dead Fabers, and wrote a message on the back of it.

He pinned it beneath a stone at the center of the trail. Then, realizing they might miss it, he hustled thirty feet back up the trail and left a string of greenbacks under similar stones.

If there was one thing men like those coming for him would notice, it was money fluttering in the breeze.

Then, knowing time was short, he climbed onto Dagger and rode to the top of the hill, where he dismounted again, tied Dagger to a tree safely down the backslope, pulled his Winchester from its boot, grabbed his saddle bags and canteen, and got into position behind the rocks at the top of the ridge.

It was a perfect setup. If he had no scruples, he could simply wait for the three riders to reach the bottom of the saddle a hundred and fifty yards downhill and knock them out of their saddles as quick as he could work the lever.

But he wasn't entirely certain that these men were Fabers, so he waited behind a sizeable boulder, watching with the spyglasses, the rifle ready on the rocky ground beside him.

He didn't have to wait long.

The three men were coming fast. He felt a twinge of sharp irritation, seeing the foaming mouths and wild eyes of their huffing steeds. They were riding these poor horses to death, that's how much they wanted to catch up with him.

Any man who'd do that to a horse… well, Justice felt like pulling the trigger right then and there.

But he held fire.

They rode right past the first two greenbacks, so great was their hurry, and he realized he might have to stop them with a warning shot.

But then one of them stopped his horse and the others hesitated, and as the man hopped down and retrieved a dollar, one of the other men shouted, pointing to another fluttering greenback.

They hopped down and picked their way forward, whooping at their luck.

Fabers or otherwise, Justice thought, *these boys are about as sharp as a sack of wet bunnies.*

And with their dark, stringy hair, wiry builds, and pointed faces, they sure did look like Fabers.

Finally, they came to the note.

One of the men picked it up and squinted dumbly at it, then crumpled it into a ball and hauled back his arm to throw it off the path, which angled sharply down on either side in a slide of scrub and scree.

But one of the other men grabbed his wrist and demanded the paper and hollered to the third man, who came over and flattened the affidavit and held it up before his eyes, studying it.

Justice watched through the spyglasses. The man's lips moved as his eyes went jerkily back and forth.

He couldn't hear the man's voice at this distance, but he could see the words forming as the man did his best to read Justice's note.

. . .

You men take the money and turn around and go back home. If you keep coming, I will assume you're coming for me and will be forced to kill all three of you.

He watched one man's eyes harden. He was the oldest of the bunch, maybe forty, whereas the other men looked to be in their twenties.

The older man's voice barked at the others.

Both men glanced up the hill to where Justice was hidden.

One shook his head.

The older man barked all the louder.

Justice couldn't make out the words, but he could still tell what was happening there, so he set down his spyglasses and picked up his rifle and got ready to go to work.

The men mounted up and argued among themselves.

The one who'd shook his head started back toward town.

The other two shucked their rifles and stood staring uphill for a moment, then spread out on the narrow trail, as if that would do them any good.

Some men were just too stupid to live. Apparently, that ran thick in the Faber clan.

The only one with a brain spurred his poor horse, hurrying back up the other side, pointed toward town.

The other two nodded, spurred their mounts, and charged uphill toward Justice, who fired, levered another round into the chamber, and fired again.

That was all she wrote for his would-be pursuers.

The fleeing man stopped near the other peak and stared back to where his kin now lay dead upon the ground.

He hesitated there, likely stunned by what had happened. But in case the man was tilting toward some senseless and suicidal charge, Justice fired again, three times, rapidly, kicking up dust in a string of panging puffs that walked up the trail to within a few feet of the stunned man.

This demonstration shook the final Faber out of his daze and apparently brought him back to his senses because he leaned over his horse, charged up the remaining slope, and disappeared over the side.

CHAPTER 41

Nora waved to Eli as the buggy pulled away, but the boy was already running off toward the barn, followed by Rafer and the pups.

She felt a twinge of concern, leaving him alone, but Eli was getting older, and Justice had taught him well, and besides, he wasn't really alone. True, Rosa was visiting her sister on her day off, and the men were out on the range, but Rafer could protect Eli better than Nora could herself.

She hoped, by leaving the boy at home, that she might be able to get Katie to finally talk about everything that happened.

The girl moped for days after Justice banished Lonnie.

Understandably, Nora thought.

Katie truly loved the boy, and Nora believed the boy loved her just as truly.

Then, the other day, after the mercantile delivery arrived, Katie grew quite cheerful for a short time.

Nora suspected that Lonnie had sent her a message through the delivery boy.

Whatever the case, Katie's happiness soon crumbled into restless anxiety.

This state concerned Nora even more than had her daughter's deep sorrow. It made her worry that Katie might be planning to do something rash.

Nora cleared her throat and dove in. "Katie, dear, how are you feeling?"

"Fine, thank you, Mama."

Nora laid her hand on Katie's. "I want to know the truth, dear. The whole truth. I love you and might understand more than you think. Please tell me how you're really feeling."

Katie turned toward her, a fake smile plastered on her face, and opened her mouth to speak. Then, blinking at Nora, the girl closed her mouth, shut her eyes, and shook her head.

When she opened her eyes again, the fake smile was long gone. "I'm sad, Mama. And worried. I... don't know what to do. I just wish I'd never hugged Lonnie. I wish Eli hadn't come around the corner. Life was so good. I had never been so happy. And then, all of the sudden, it was horrible. Pa was so mad, and... I just wish... I wish he hadn't kicked Lonnie out. I wish things could be like they were."

"I do, too, sweetie. I do, too."

"You do?"

Nora nodded. "It was nice seeing you so happy. And Lonnie seems like a good boy."

"He is, Mama. He really is. I love him so much."

"I know you do, honey."

"Could you talk to Pa? Could you tell him that you think Lonnie is a good man?"

Nora frowned. "That isn't as easy as it sounds, Katie."

"Does Pa hate him that much?"

"No, he doesn't hate Lonnie. In fact, I think he was starting to warm up to him, which isn't easy for your pa."

"Why?"

"Because he loves you. He doesn't want anyone to hurt you."

Katie was silent for a moment. Then she nodded.

"I know Pa loves me, and I'll always be so thankful to both of you for saving and adopting me, but sometimes…"

Nora waited, giving the girl time.

"Sometimes, I wonder if Pa will ever let me be happy."

"You're not happy at home?"

"I am. That's not what I mean. But… with Lonnie, I was happier than I had ever been. It was so exciting, talking with him. Now, it feels like I'll never be happy again, not without Lonnie."

"You're young, Katie."

"But I mean it. I mean it all. It's real, Mama."

"I know it is, dear. I understand what you're saying and feeling. I don't mean to say it isn't real. I just mean to say that life is hard on the young sometimes. Right now, you can't see any happiness without Lonnie, but that's just not true, dear. There could be other boys. You might—"

Katie shook her head. "No, ma'am. I won't ever love another. Lonnie is the only man I will ever love. Besides, even if there was another, it wouldn't work. If Pa won't let me see a good man like Lonnie, who would he let me see?"

"We're all new at this, dear. This is your first time falling in love, and it's the first time your pa has had a daughter fall in love. He's trying to protect you."

"He ruined everything. With Lonnie, I was so happy."

"So happy that you hugged him. And Eli thought you were kissing."

"We weren't! I swear!"

"I believe you. I believe Eli made a mistake. But he never would have made the mistake if you hadn't made a mistake first."

Katie nodded miserably.

"And your pa never would have reacted the way he did if both you and Eli hadn't made mistakes."

"I know, Mama. I'm sorry. I know Pa loves me. I just… I just wish I could go back. I wish I could make things right."

"Well, maybe you can."

Katie's eyes brightened. "How? We can't go back in time."

"No, but we might still set things right. Your pa has had a hard time with this, but he loves you, Katie, and wants what's best for you. When men see problems, they like to solve them quickly and completely. But sometimes, they need time. Maybe when your pa gets back, we'll be able to talk to him. Maybe he'll give Lonnie a second chance."

Katie clasped her hand. "Do you really think so, Mama? Do you think he'll let Lonnie come back?"

"I can't say for sure, Katie. I just wouldn't give up hope yet."

"I won't, Mama. Thank you so much for talking with me about this. I've been so lonely since everything happened. When you tried to talk, I wanted to—I really did—but I was afraid that you would just tell me to forget about Lonnie. I won't ever do that."

Nora nodded. She understood that Katie's youthful devotion was blinding her, but now wasn't the time to mention this.

Sometimes, what you say is less important than what you have the sense not to.

That went double for parenting. And triple, Nora was beginning to understand, for parenting teenage girls.

They were silent for several seconds.

Then Katie said, "Mama, do you think I could maybe stop by the livery in Dos Pesos? I sure would like to see Lonnie, even if for just a minute."

Nora smiled. She had been expecting this and had lost some sleep considering her response.

She had meant what she'd said to Katie. It was possible that Justice would give Lonnie another chance.

Otherwise, Nora would forbid the meeting.

But if she did forbid a brief reunion, she was afraid the young lovers might try to elope. A young, capable cowboy with a horse and money could certainly make that happen.

She wanted Katie to know things could still work out, that she might be able to stay with her family without losing Lonnie.

So she said, "Yes, dear. You may see him."

"Thank you, Mama." Katie bit her lip. "Do you think maybe I could talk to him alone?"

"You're not thinking of doing anything rash, are you?"

Katie tilted her head, looking puzzled. "No, Mama. I just want to be able to talk privately with him is all."

It was a risk, Nora knew, allowing such a meeting, but she had to have faith that things would work out and that, after many prayers for guidance, God was directing her paths.

"Okay, sweetie. I trust you. When I go to the bank to pick up money for the payroll, you may go to the livery and speak privately with Lonnie."

Katie leaned across the seat and hugged Nora gently around the middle. "Oh, thank you, Mama. Thank you so much. You don't know what this means to me."

CHAPTER 42

Once they had hitched the horse in front of the bank and parted, it was all Katie could do not to pick up her skirts and run all the way to the livery.

How surprised Lonnie would be to see her!

Her heart hammered with anticipation.

Going through the door, she nervously tucked an errant lock behind her ear. She'd never felt so nervous and excited in all her life!

But where was Lonnie?

Probably back with the horses.

What if he wasn't here? What if Mr. Chavez had sent him on an errand? Or what if today was Lonnie's day off, and he was off in the mountains, riding?

Mr. Chavez came in from the back. Seeing her, the hostler smiled broadly. "Well, hello, Katie. It's nice to see you. Is your father back in town?"

"Not yet, Mr. Chavez."

"Always feel safer when he is."

"Yes, sir. Is Lonnie here, sir?"

Mr. Chavez looked troubled for a second. "Yes, he's working today."

"Would it be possible for me to see him for just a minute, please, Mr. Chavez?"

"Does your mother know you're here?"

"Yes, sir. She's over at the bank. She said it was okay if I spoke with Lonnie."

Mr. Chavez seemed to relax a little, and Katie realized he'd probably been worried about angering her pa, who had quite a reputation in town.

Mr. Chavez went into the back. She heard his voice calling for Lonnie.

Katie took a deep breath and clasped her hands together to keep them from shaking.

A moment later, Lonnie appeared in the door.

Her heart hopped with joy.

A huge smile broke across Lonnie's handsome face as he stepped forward. "Katie!"

"Hi, Lonnie. Sorry to surprise you at work."

"Sorry?" he laughed. "This is wonderful. I'm happier than a boardinghouse pup. But how did you get here?"

"Mama's at the bank. I told her how I felt, and she said I could come over and talk to you."

He took a few steps forward and stood there, smiling down at her, close enough to touch. "Your pa in town, too?"

She shook her head. "He's out on the trail."

"Out tracking bad men."

She shrugged. "I suppose."

"I sure do admire him. I wish things were different."

"So do I, Lonnie. So do I." She had the wild urge to hug him again, but remembering how much trouble that had brought them last time, she restrained herself. "Thank you so much for the sweet letter."

He grinned. "You got it, huh?"

She nodded. "It made me awful happy."

"Good. I'm glad, Katie. I meant every word. I love you, and I ain't never gonna stop loving you no matter what."

"And I'll never stop loving you, Lonnie. Mama says maybe, if she talks to him, that Pa might reconsider."

Lonnie beamed at the news. "Do you really think so?"

She nodded, realizing she did believe it could happen. She trusted Mama, and knew Pa loved her dearly. Besides, seeing Lonnie again made her feel like anything was possible. "I really do. I—"

Gunshots boomed out in the street.

She gasped, turning for the door, but Lonnie beat her to it.

Looking outside, he said, "Something's going on over at the bank."

"Mama!" Katie cried.

CHAPTER 43

E arlier, as a very happy Katie hurried off toward the livery, Nora, not noticing the riders coming slowly up the street, entered the Dos Pesos Bank, feeling pretty good about the way things had gone.

It was so difficult to know what to say or do in a moment like that. For days, she had struggled to be a good mother to Katie.

Perhaps it would've been easier, or at least more natural, for her to counsel the young woman if she had raised Katie from birth, but she doubted it.

This was a difficult situation. That was all. And even if she had raised Katie from birth, even if she'd been her flesh and blood, the situation would be the same. Katie would still be gushing with emotion and still hobbled by the strange imagination of a sixteen-year-old, which allowed her to believe she'd found the perfect love of her life while simultaneously refusing to believe there could be anyone else in the future.

She smiled to herself, thinking this was a problem millions of mothers, including her own, had faced at one time or another.

Things would be okay.

She would talk to Justice, and yes, things would be okay.

"Hello, Mrs. Bullard," Stuart Gable, the teller, said, smiling at her from his window. "Always a pleasure to see you."

"Thank you, Mister Gable. And likewise." She meant it. Gable was nice, even if he was prone to gossip. "I hope you are doing well?"

"Yes, ma'am. What can I help you with today?"

"The end of the month is coming up. I want to withdraw money for payroll and other expenses."

"Yes, ma'am. I'll be happy to help you with that." He pushed a slip through the window and smiled. "Speaking of payroll, I hear a rumor that you've taken on another employee."

"That's right. Rosa is cooking for us now."

Gable leaned a little closer, glanced to the left and right, and whispered conspiratorially, "I heard that—"

Whatever he'd been about to say was lost when the front door banged open, and several men with drawn weapons flooded into the bank, led by a short, broad-shouldered man in a sombrero.

This man spat a smoking cigar onto the floor and offered a sneering smile. "We have come here to relieve you of your money!"

Nora's mind reeled with terror.

Because she recognized these men from the wanted posters Justice had shared.

The Undergrove Gang had come to Dos Pesos.

Instinctively, her hand fell to her pocket where she always carried the derringer Justice had given her.

But even as her fingers closed on the pocket pistol, she realized the folly of trying anything against several armed killers, especially at this distance.

A split-second later, as if to punctuate her line of thinking, the bank erupted in gunfire.

Terrified, Nora went to the ground and lay on her side, careful not to bump the baby against the floor.

The shooting was over quickly. Her ears rang. Gunsmoke hung heavily in the air, filling her nostrils with a familiar smell she generally associated with her husband.

Only now, her husband was far, far away... chasing this very gang, ironically.

These thoughts flitted through her mind with the speed of terror, and glancing to her left, she saw Mr. Alvarado lying there and knew instantly that he would never rise again.

Behind the counter, someone was moaning in pain.

One of the robbers, a burly man with his head shaved to dark stubble, walked over, stuck his hat through the window, then quickly leaned in with a pistol and fired three shots.

The moaning stopped.

All that was left was the sound of weeping here and there.

Nora concentrated on her breathing, trying to stave off panic.

As Justice always said, the most important survival skill this side of preparedness was staying calm.

"Next one of you who screams gets what they got," the man in the sombrero announced.

Undergrove, she told herself. *That's the gang leader, Cyrus Undergrove.*

"The bank manager has three seconds to get out here with his hands up," Undergrove declared.

A second later, Percy Littlefield stood up behind the counter with his hands lifted high. "I am the bank manager, sir."

"Get the vault open now," Undergrove told him.

Mr. Littlefield unlocked the vault and retrieved the money.

Gang members moved forward and seized the money sacks.

"Everybody in the vault," Undergrove commanded, studying the frightened patrons and tellers.

Nora came cautiously to her feet, new horror rising in her as she remembered everything about Undergrove, about how every time he robbed a bank, he took—

"You," Undergrove told Nora, a nasty smile spreading across his unshaven face. "You're coming with me."

CHAPTER 44

The words froze her blood. He had chosen her, just as he had chosen those other women. "But sir, please, I'm pregnant."

He grabbed her arm in a painful grip. "Don't worry, ma'am. It won't be but a short trip."

"Here comes the sheriff and a couple others," a man near the door reported as Undergrove drug Nora toward the door.

"Ain't that heroic?" Undergrove chuckled. "Trouble with being a hero is, heroes die."

Outside, a loud rifle fired three times rapidly.

Undergrove shoved through the door and dragged Nora out onto the front steps of the bank, where she saw three men on the ground and another on a rooftop across the street, holding a rifle and scanning the street.

Then, with a jolt of terror, she saw Katie coming out of the livery. In front of her, his long blond hair trailing behind him like a cape, Lonnie ran with his gun drawn, sprinting straight at the trouble.

The man on the roof swung his eyes in that direction.

"Lonnie!" Nora screamed. "Look out on the roof!"

She pointed to where the man was raising the rifle to his shoulder, and a tremendous blow clouted her in the temple, filling her head with sparks and making her legs go weak.

Undergrove cursed at her. "Another word out of you, you're dead!"

As he spoke, gunshots erupted.

As Nora steadied herself, she stared in wonder, watching the rifleman's limp body plummet from the rooftop and crunch into the street below.

Lonnie had done it, he'd shot the man off the roof, from that distance, with a pistol!

Now, the boy was rushing forward, straight at them. "You let Mrs. Bullard go!" Lonnie shouted, firing his pistol.

The gang opened up on the boy as he charged.

One of the gang members dropped. Then another.

Lonnie jerked and hunched as if an invisible fist had punched him in the stomach.

Somehow, as such miracles sometimes occur in life-and-death moments, Nora was aware of her daughter's voice screaming Lonnie's name from down the street, where she was being restrained by the hostler, Mr. Chavez.

Lonnie fired again, and Undergrove jerked, roaring with pain, and released Nora.

Nora saw Lonnie get struck again, his shoulder snapping backward in a red mist, and still again, one leg folding unnaturally beneath him.

Lonnie dropped to the ground.

Undergrove, wincing in pain, grabbed for her arm.

Nora pulled her pocket pistol and fired at her would-be killer.

Undergrove's head jerked, the side of his face spraying blood. He staggered backward and fell onto the seat of his britches.

Nora turned and ran.

Behind her, Undergrove spewed curses. His pistol roared and roared again, and Nora heard something whiz through the air, passing mere inches from her ear.

Then she was behind a wagon. No, a buggy. Her own buggy. And she remembered the shotgun.

Justice hid weapons everywhere, and always kept a 12-gauge, double-barreled coach gun under the seat of the buggy.

Leaning into the buggy, she seized the weapon and slid its twin barrels over the seat, ready to return fire.

But she couldn't pull the triggers, because Undergrove had taken another hostage, schoolteacher Jenny Walton, and was riding off with his surviving gang members down the street, disappearing into a cloud of dust.

CHAPTER 45

J ustice woke early and went to the windows and studied the predawn gloom for any sign of danger.

Instead of heading on to Bernalillo, he had left the trail and cut across the east, picking up another road and following it north to this little village.

He doubted the Fabers would follow and didn't think they could find him even if they did. It would take a special kind of tracker to follow his trail through the scrub on a cloudy night.

But here he was, only half a day's ride from home, when he was supposed to be further south, hunting the Undergrove Gang.

Oh well. He'd done good work with Prima and the Fabers, and he'd taken a lesson to heart.

After sleeping on it, he reckoned he should've talked to Katie. He still thought he'd done the right thing, sending the boy away, but one way or the other, when he got home, he planned on sitting her down and letting her have her say.

What's more, he planned on listening.

Then they'd see.

He did not want to follow in Prima's footsteps.

That didn't mean he'd give Katie whatever she wanted. That would be parenting at its worst.

After all, a spoiled child never loves her parents.

So no, he wouldn't just give Katie whatever she wanted, but he would hear her out with an open mind and a loving heart.

That was the best he could do, and he sure hoped it was enough.

Before heading home, however, he still needed to ride south, search for clues concerning the Undergrove Gang, and warn lawmen and bankers along the way.

He got around and checked his weapons and carried everything downstairs, where he paid his bill and warned the innkeeper about the Undergrove Gang.

Then he went next door to the café and waited to order breakfast.

A moment later, the innkeeper showed up wearing an apron.

"Good morning, sir. What can I get for you?"

Justice ordered fried eggs, sausage, home fries, and coffee.

The innkeeper went into the back and came back out with a steaming cup of coffee. "Your food'll be right up, sir. Won't take but a minute."

"Thank you," Justice said, and when the man left, Justice rose and crossed the room and picked up the newspaper someone had left spread atop an abandoned table.

He carried the paper back to his seat, took a sip of piping-hot coffee, folded the paper shut, and read the headline with a jolt of apprehension.

BANK ROBBER BLOODBATH IN DOS PESOS!

INSIDE JUSTICE, SOMETHING TIGHTENED LIKE A FIST AS HE READ, "The *notorious Undergrove Gang struck again yesterday afternoon, this time in the small town of Dos Pesos, New Mexico, getting away with thousands of dollars and leaving more than a dozen dead or wounded in their wake, including four of Undergrove's men, thanks to the heroics of Lonnie Cooper, 17, of Dos Pesos, who also fell in the melee.*"

Justice's eyes flashed over the article, seeing other familiar names.

Then his guts clamped into a tight fist as he read the line, "Also injured in the incident were Nora Bullard, 24, of Dos Pesos, and—"

Justice shoved a hand into his pocket, spilled some coins on the table, and ran out the door.

The next few hours, he prayed like he'd never prayed before, these prayers living in stark juxtaposition with the murderous rage that had fallen over him like a dark cloak.

He was going to kill Cyrus Undergrove and all his men.

But first, he needed to get home, needed to see Nora, needed to make sure she was all right.

He rode hard, stopping at a ranch along the way and buying a horse so he could rest Dagger then swap back to his stallion when the new horse started to flag.

The closer he got to home, the more his fear grew.

Was Nora okay?

Was the baby all right?

CHAPTER 46

Reaching home, Justice raced past the pups and Rafer, dismounted at the house, and rushed inside, where a stunned-looking Eli reflexively turned a shotgun on him.

The boy's eyes swelled, and he turned the barrel aside. "Pa! You're home. Sorry I pointed the gun at you."

"Don't apologize, son," Justice said, leaning to hug the boy. "Those were good instincts. Where's your mama?"

"I'm here," Nora said, appearing in the hallway. She looked a little haggard, but she smiled, coming into his arms.

"You're okay?"

"Yes. A bit shaken, but okay."

"And the baby?"

She laid a hand on her stomach. "The baby is fine."

"Praise God for that."

"Oh, I have. Many, many times. And speaking of prayers of thanks, I am so glad you're home."

He held her tightly. "I'm so sorry I wasn't here to protect you."

"Don't feel that way, Justice. You were out doing your job, chasing down these exact men. You couldn't have known they were coming here."

He knew she was right, but the fact that he hadn't been here for his family would haunt him forever.

Thoughts of family raised fresh fear within him. "Wait. Where's Katie? Is she okay?"

"Yes, she's okay. She's next door in the guesthouse, nursing Lonnie."

"He's alive? The paper wasn't clear."

Nora nodded. "He's alive. It was a close thing yesterday, and how he survived, I'll never know. It was a miracle, Justice, a miracle. He saved my life. Gunned down a whole bunch of the robbers. They shot him all to pieces, but he just kept fighting until finally a bullet busted his leg and put him down. Even then, practically bleeding out, he laid there, reloading, hoping to shoot them as they raced out of town. I've never seen anything like it."

Justice hugged her again, taking it all in as he checked her for any injuries he'd missed.

"Justice, they—Undergrove—he took me hostage…"

He hugged her again. "I read about it in the paper. I'm so sorry, Nora, and I'm so thankful you're okay."

Once he was sure she was all right, he hurried next door to see Katie and the boy who'd saved Nora.

Lonnie lay in the bedroom sleeping, his colorless face slack within the halo of pale blond hair that stuck out from beneath the bloody bandages covering the top of his skull.

More bandages encased his left shoulder and long torso. His right side sported a large, dark bloodstain.

His leg, also bandaged and bloody, was elevated, the bottom of the splint propped up onto the footboard.

From a chair beside the bed, Katie came to her feet. Her dress was bloodstained, her hair stuck out in all directions, and her eyes were red and swollen from crying. It was instantly clear to him that she'd stayed up all night, watching over Lonnie.

She didn't even bother with a hello. "Don't you tell me to leave him, Pa, because I'd rather die."

"Katie, sweetie, I'm sorry," he said. "I won't tell you to leave him, honey. Okay? You stick by his side."

He moved in and took her in his arms, and she hugged him fiercely, crying again.

"I was so afraid, Daddy," she said. It was the first time she'd ever called him that, and somehow it made her seem younger and more vulnerable. "I've been so afraid."

"It's okay, sweetie. You're okay. Everything's going to be okay."

"Everything's going to be okay?"

"Yes, I promise. Everything's going to be all right. I'm going to fix everything."

He could feel her small head twisting back and forth against his chest. "Not possible. How could anybody fix—"

"Shh, sweetheart. Shh. Everything's gonna be all right. I promise." He rubbed her back. "I love you, Katie, and I'm so glad you're okay. You take good care of this boy, and we'll talk about the two of you when I get back."

Katie stepped back with an incredulous expression twisting

her exhausted features. "Get back? You're leaving again? Mama needs you. We all need you. What could possibly be important enough to pull you away at a time like this?"

Justice stared into her eyes and said nothing for a full three seconds. "I'm going to kill the men who did this, sweetie. I'm going to track them down and kill every last one of them and stop them from hurting anyone else ever again."

Katie blinked at him, then glanced at Lonnie and smoothed a hand lovingly over his golden locks.

When she turned her gaze back on Justice, she was no longer crying.

"Do it, Daddy. Kill them. Kill them all."

CHAPTER 47

Cyrus Undergrove took a slug of whiskey, listening to the others bellyache. He hadn't spoken in a long time, and Frank Wyatt, wary as always, was looking at him sideways, as if expecting Cyrus to blow up like a stick of dynamite.

Donnie Reese, who everybody called Slick, had been whining ever since they holed up here in the mountains southwest of Dos Pesos. Now, Slick sat there licking his lips nervously and looking back and forth between the twins, Bo and Hardy Bannerman, who were complaining again about the other kid, the one who'd shot Cyrus in the side and gunned down four gang members, including Hank Hardesty.

How the blasted kid had managed to nail Hardesty from that distance with a pistol, Cyrus would never know.

Nor did it matter, since they'd put the kid down.

"I just can't believe it," Hardy grumbled. "What kind of a kid fights like that? Those were good men he put down."

"Deekins wasn't much good," Bo countered, the two of them forever compelled to contradict one another.

Hardy made a face. "Deek could fight. Why, one time, I seen him take out three Mexicans all at the same time. They was—"

"That kid was the woman's girl's boyfriend, that's what the hostage said," Slick said, his boyish face and frightened eyes making him look like a little kid listening to ghost stories around a campfire. "That's what the schoolteacher said. Said that other woman, Bullard or whatever, the one that nearly did for Cyrus, it was her daughter's boyfriend."

Everybody fell silent for a second.

"Maybe the husband taught that kid how to fight," Hardy said. "The bounty hunter."

Bo spat a long stream of tobacco juice onto the rocks in front of the cave. "I doubt it," he said in an obligatory contradiction that didn't have much punch.

Frank Wyatt was always paranoid, but now, his eyes gleamed with the fear that made him so dangerous. "I'll bet that's where the kid learned to fight. That bounty hunter taught him. According to what that schoolteacher said."

"Forget what that schoolteacher said," Cyrus growled, and everybody shut up.

How he wished he'd never chosen that schoolteacher. He should've shot her as soon as she'd started laughing like crazy and gloating about how they'd messed with the wrong woman. Not her, but the pregnant one, the one who'd shot his ear off and burned his cheek, that Nora Bullard.

Don't you know who her husband is, you fools? the schoolteacher had laughed gleefully. *He's Justice Bullard, the best bounty hunter in New Mexico Territory. You're all dead men.*

Her wild eyes had flicked from one to the other.

You're all dead. You just don't know it yet.

Cyrus had cuffed her then. His ear and face were killing him. He wanted to shoot her just to shut her up. But he kept her alive a little bit longer until she told him everything he wanted to know about the Bullards.

Then he had very happily blown a hole through her head.

The men were all staring at him now.

"How is one man gonna come and get all of us?" he demanded.

Slick spoke up. "According to that schoolteacher—"

Cyrus lurched forward and slapped Slick across the chops. "I told you to shut up about that woman."

Slick dropped a hand to his gun butt.

Cyrus smiled. "You want to try it? Go ahead, Slick. You go ahead and try to draw, and I'll smash this whiskey bottle over your head before you can clear leather."

Knowing Slick wouldn't dare to draw on him, Cyrus got to his feet. "What's wrong with you boys? We just pulled off the score of a lifetime, and you're moping like a bunch of babies. Thirty thousand dollars. Six thousand dollars apiece. That's big money in case you forgot."

The men nodded and studied their boots.

Then Bo said, "Yeah, but we left four men back there."

"So what? That was their fault, not ours. They were the ones dumb enough to die, not us. So now we got their shares."

"I still say we shoulda run south," Hardy grumbled.

"Shouldn't be sitting here, not even ten miles from town," Bo said, almost agreeing with his brother.

"That's exactly what they expected us to do," Cyrus said.

"Better to hole up here, see what's what, and then slip away to Mexico."

"I'm sick of Mexico," Slick mumbled.

"Then stay here," Cyrus said.

Slick shook his head.

"The faster we get to Mexico, the better," Wyatt said and cast a sour look around the kitchen. "I hate this place, hate sitting here, drinking coffee. Feels like we're waiting on company. And ain't but one type of visitor's gonna show up here."

"A posse," McCavitt said.

"Or that bounty hunter," Slick said and licked his upper lip.

Wyatt nodded grimly. "Could be. Could just be. I say we move out at dusk, head south at a clip, stick to the scrub, and shoot anybody who so much as says howdy."

"We'd be dead by noon tomorrow," Hardy said with characteristic swagger then shot Cyrus a bitter look approaching a challenge. "We screwed up, sticking around. Shoulda lit straight out. But now the country's crawling with lawmen."

"Forget the lawmen," Bo said. "It's the locals that got me laying low. They're all hunters in this country. I say we sit tight, let things simmer down. We got everything we need right here. Food, water, whiskey. We'd even have a woman if Hardy'd had the sense to tie her up."

Slick shuddered. "I went in there this morning, saw her laying there with her wrists slit and her eyes wide open. It was like she was staring straight at me, like she was a ghost or something. Looking at me like hey, buddy, I will have my revenge."

The twins laughed at that.

Wyatt clutched his gut, looking more worried than ever. "Let's get out of here."

McCavitt nodded. "I'm with Wyatt. Let's shoot our way back to Old Mexico and retire in style."

"What do you think, Cyrus?" Slick asked and licked his lip again.

Moving slowly, Cyrus took his boots down off the table and placed them firmly on the ground.

He'd been biding his time, letting them talk and fret and squabble, letting them come to the conclusions he'd already known they would come to.

Now, it was time to drive the wedge.

"Here's what I'm gonna do," he said, and told them his plan. Well, at least up to the point that he would betray them and take their gold.

Which was why he needed the wedge. Five was too many. Three, now… three would be perfect.

Slick might defect out of fear, but he didn't think so.

"You gotta be crazy if you think we're gonna do that," Hardy growled.

"You go ahead and get yourselves killed," Bo said. "Me and Hardy'll sit right here."

Cyrus sipped his whiskey and looked from one twin to the other. "You two are quitting the gang?"

Hardy's eyes flared a little. "Look, Cyrus. We don't want no bad blood with you. It's just—"

"Bad blood?" Cyrus said. "No way. You boys want out, I ain't gonna try to stop you."

Bo leaned back with a leery expression. "That's what you told Bradshaw. Now his bones are bleaching in the sun."

"Ben Bradshaw was a snake," Cyrus said. "I was fixing to let him leave, but he stole my cigars. Look, boys, we been riding together a long time. You want out, go ahead. You won't even have to leave. You just sit tight. We're leaving... now."

He turned to the others. "You boys ready?"

Wyatt nodded.

McCavitt stood. "Ready, boss."

Cyrus turned his gaze on Slick, who licked his lip, looking back and forth between Cyrus and the twins.

"You gonna sit here and die?" Cyrus asked him. "Or ride with us to freedom and fortune?"

Slick hesitated. For someone so quick with a shooting iron, Cyrus thought, he sure was a gutless turd.

"Come on, kid," McCavitt said, clapping Slick on the shoulder. "Cyrus got us this far. Might as well trust him to get us home again."

Slick nodded. "All right. Yeah. All right. I'll come with you."

Cyrus nodded and made a show of shaking hands with Hardy and Bo. Not for their benefit. He didn't care what the twins thought. If he ever got the chance, he'd dry gulch the pair of them and leave them for buzzard bait, the cowards.

But he put on a show of good will for the benefit of the men still riding with him.

It would be better this way. Robbing banks, you needed a big crew. Running, big numbers brought trouble. Made you stand out.

Plus, with the twins gone, it'd be easier to do what he had to do. With only Slick, Wyatt, and McCavitt along, he could quadruple his fortune.

Shooting three men in their bedrolls would be easy, after all.

Five, on the other hand, you try shooting five men in their sleep, and one or two might get a shot off, might even kill you.

But three would be easy, especially when they didn't suspect a thing.

"You boys take care," he said, shaking the twins' hands again. "Hope to see you on the other side."

The other men seemed happy with the parting.

Good. He still needed them.

Let them help him back to Mexico. Then he'd kill them in their sleep and live like a king.

Maybe he'd even take that woman with him.

He lifted a hand to the mess that had only recently been his ear.

Yeah, that was just what he'd do.

CHAPTER 48

J ustice started in Dos Pesos, learned everything he could as quickly as he could, then headed back out, following the outlaws' trail west into the mountains until he lost it.

From there, he descended to a sandy wash and rode south, cutting for sign.

He picked up their tracks again where they headed into the river valley and was cutting across Greg Kipling's land when he spotted a posse led by none other than Kipling himself.

The men nodded grimly.

"Real sorry about what happened, Justice," Pedro Esteban said. "How's Mrs. Bullard?"

"She's all right."

"How about the kid?" Greg Kipling asked.

"Lonnie's tough as a nickel steak," Justice said. "I reckon he'll pull through."

"He was shot all to pieces," one man said.

One of Kipling's hands nodded. "Heard he killed four of them outlaws. Must be quite the scrapper."

"Look, men," Justice said. "I gotta find Undergrove. Have you seen anything?"

"Not a thing," Kipling said mournfully.

Justice didn't bother to mention the tracks he'd been following. These men were ranchers, not trackers, and he didn't know any of them well enough to trust them in a fight like this. "Did you notice anything strange?"

Their confusion showed plainly on their faces.

"Anything strange at all?" Justice explained. "Did anything make you look twice? Did anything seem out of place? Anything at all?"

They thought for a moment and shook their heads.

Except for Esteban, who said, "Well, there is one thing."

"What's that?"

"Leonard didn't show up."

Justice waited while the other men started nodding.

"Leonard Gammons said he'd ride with us. But he went home and never showed at the rendezvous point. That's not like him."

Justice knew Gammons well enough to understand what Esteban meant. Gammons was one of those neat and tidy ranchers who never went to town without putting on a starched shirt. He rode high-stepping Arabians that always looked like they were on their way to a horse show.

Say what you want about gentleman ranchers like Gammons, but men who iron their jeans do tend to honor their promises.

Justice thanked the posse and said maybe he'd pay Gammons a visit.

"Want us to ride along, Justice?" Kipling asked.

"No thanks," Justice said. He appreciated these men coming out and hunting, but they were not killers. And against a gang like Undergrove's, a man would have to kill or die. It was as simple as that.

And Justice was ready to kill.

He rode off south, not bothering to go back to the tracks he'd been following, reckoning his path would converge with theirs soon, anyway.

And sure enough, as he was entering the Gammons place, he picked up the riders' trail again.

He slowed to a walk and branched away from the tracks, which headed straight for the ranch house.

Justice circled around back, got behind the buildings, and dismounted within a grove of live oaks shading a small cemetery.

Hitching the bay there, he slung his Winchester over one shoulder and moved slowly toward the stable, careful to keep his elbow between the rifle stock and that of the eight gauge, which he carried at the ready.

Before leaving the trees, he spent a good fifteen minutes watching and listening. He could only see one corner of the house. Nothing was moving.

He hustled across open ground to the stable. Before going inside, he saw the line of fresh tracks leading away past the house and felt a stab of disappointment.

But studying them further, he realized there weren't enough tracks for the whole gang. At least, it didn't seem that way.

Which meant some of them might still be inside.

He entered the stable and discovered a pair of dirty and disheveled geldings with Army brands that had no business among the neatly groomed Arabians of Leonard Gammons.

The geldings probably belonged to the twins, Bo and Hardy Bannerman, a pair of big outlaws who last year had wiped out a six-man army patrol that had scouted too close to their hideout in Texas.

Moving to the front of the stable, Justice watched the house. At one point, he thought he saw movement through one of the kitchen windows, but he wasn't certain.

Other than that, all was still.

He'd grabbed the Winchester 73 when he thought he might end up facing the whole gang. In a situation like that, when pausing to reload could get a man killed, he might need all fifteen rounds in the Winchester's tube magazine.

But now that he realized he was only facing the twins, he leaned the lever-action out of sight inside the stable door, knowing he needed mobility, stealth, and raw, close-quarters power now.

He ran from the stable to the privy, where he paused again, listening and watching. Again, he saw movement in the kitchen, so he worked his way around to the back of the house and tried the door.

It was locked.

Listening hard, ready for anything, he crept along the house until he came to another door.

This time, the knob turned easily.

Holding his breath, he opened the door silently and stood there with his shotgun at the ready.

He stepped into the tiled hallway, walking on the balls of his feet. One scuff at a moment like this could get him killed.

The place was neat and tidy save for where the gang had tracked a bunch of mud across the floor.

Voices drifted back from the other end of the house.

"Gonna get themselves killed," a man's voice said.

"Shame to lose all that money."

"Should've plugged them and taken it."

"Had it just been Cyrus, I would've."

"I don't know. He's quicker than he looks."

"Not as quick as Slick."

"No, maybe not, but who'd win a fight between them?"

"Cyrus."

"There you go."

Justice moved along the hall, approaching an open doorway that, if he wasn't mistaken, either opened into a huge kitchen or another hallway that would lead him to the kitchen.

"Know what I think?" one of the voices said.

"I got no idea."

"I think we'd best get out of here."

"What are you talking about, Hardy? What happened to laying low?"

"What do you think's gonna happen if one of them boys gets taken alive? They'll roll over quicker than a spotted pup."

"And tell everybody exactly where we're at."

"Which is why we gotta move."

"Where to? I meant what I said. This country's crawling with posses."

"Don't have to go far. Find another ranch. One with a living, breathing woman."

Justice stepped into the doorway, ready to pull both triggers, but it wasn't the kitchen. It was just a hallway leading to the other end of the house.

He could see the doorway to the kitchen standing open down there to the right.

Their voices came through it, louder and clearer than before.

He moved in that direction.

"I like the sounds of that, brother. Have some fun while we're laying low, then get out of here once things quiet down. I sure don't want to tangle with that bounty hunter. They say he killed Oliver Rose."

"Yeah right. You believe that?"

"You should," Justice said, stepping into the doorway. "I did kill him."

One of the twins was standing there. The other sat at the table, drinking whiskey.

They both hollered with surprise.

The one standing there went for his pistol, while the other one knocked his chair over jumping to his feet.

Justice pulled one trigger, filling the room with noise, and introduced the standing brother's face to a load of buckshot.

As the other brother slapped leather, Justice turned and lowered his barrel some and pulled the other trigger.

The surviving twin's legs kicked out from under him, and he screamed and dropped hard, and his six-shooter went sliding across the bloody tiles.

Justice tossed his shotgun onto the counter, pulled a Colt, and put it on the screaming man.

"Just shoot me," Bannerman groaned, clutching his perforated pelvis. "Put me out of my misery."

"Normally, I'd tie you and let you suffer. It's what you deserve. You killed good people, hurt my wife, shot one of my hired hands, and stole my money. And I have a feeling you killed the Gammons family, too."

"Only the rancher. The wife done herself in after we all used her."

Justice tried not to think of Martha Gammons, a nice woman he'd met only twice, and the suffering she must have endured at the hands of these cruel outlaws. He pushed her from his mind, which had latched onto this current moment with the hard, cold teeth of a bear trap.

"But I'll make you a deal you don't deserve. You tell me where to find Undergrove, I'll put a bullet through your head."

Bannerman shook his head, wincing with the pain. "I might've come to a bad end, but I never was no traitor."

"Not like Undergrove, huh?" Justice chuckled, preparing the crucial lie. "He sure did stab you and your brother in the back."

"What are you talking about?"

"How do you think I found you so quick?"

"How?"

"Cyrus Undergrove. He told me where to find you."

"Figures. You kill him?"

"Haven't caught him yet. Didn't need to. He nailed a note to the front gate outside then told three different folks where to find you." Justice laughed, grinding it into the lie like salt into a wound.

Bannerman cursed Undergrove up one side and down the other, clearly puzzled why the man would betray him.

"Guess Undergrove thought he'd buy some time, giving you up like that. Probably hoped you'd get lucky and kill me."

"Get that bullet ready, bounty hunter, because I'm fixing to tell you exactly where Cyrus is headed. Cyrus always takes a hostage. He'd use his own women and children as a shield. But not with you chasing him, not when he can just use your wife and kids instead."

Bannerman pointed at Justice and laughed nastily, draining blood from his mouth.

Always a man to keep his promises, Justice pulled the trigger, grabbed his shotgun, and fled the house.

CHAPTER 49

Cyrus lowered the spyglass and grinned. He and his crew were tucked back in a clump of trees a few hundred yards from the ranch house.

Of course, he had no idea a man named Del Mundo had not long ago used the same cover for similar work.

"Well, I've seen enough. There's no men here. The idiots are probably all out hunting us." He laughed. "The hens are all home, and there ain't a watchdog in sight."

"Can I look through the scope?" Slick asked.

Cyrus ignored him, collapsing the brass tube and tucking it into his jacket pocket. "Slick, you go get that kid."

"The one on the horse?"

"That's right. Go get him."

"I don't know where he went."

"You saw just as well as I did where he went. Down that way by the river."

"Brush looks awful heavy down there."

"Are you telling me you're scared of a little kid?"

"He had a rifle in that saddle scabbard. He might hole up in that scrub and plug me is all I'm saying. We take them women, what do we even need the kid for?"

"Shut up and do as you're told, Slick. He's a kid. Take him. I can't be the only one who wants a shield."

Wyatt and McCavitt nodded, understanding, and Slick spat on the ground. "All right, all right. I'll get the kid. But if he shoots at me, I'll kill him."

"Show him who's boss," Cyrus laughed. "You're mean as a snake and twice as dumb, Slick. Go get that kid. We'll grab the women and meet you back here."

Slick hurried off through the trees toward the river.

"What about us, boss?" Wyatt asked.

"The wife's down there in the main house. She's mine. The daughter's next door in the guesthouse. You boys get her. No man will shoot someone holding his daughter."

Wyatt nodded. "All right, boss. We'll get her."

But McCavitt's mouth fell open, and he pointed at a dust cloud in the distance. "Rider coming, Cyrus."

Cyrus grinned again. "That'll be our bounty hunter. Let's go."

Wyatt unslung his rifle. "Why not just shoot him when he gets here?"

Cyrus spat with disgust. "And give these women a chance to hole up with rifles? Don't be an idiot. Come on, let's take these hostages."

CHAPTER 50

K atie smoothed a hand over Lonnie's hair again.
He opened his eyes and smiled weakly up at her.
"You sure are pretty, Katie."

She laughed, fighting back tears yet again. What was wrong
with her? Would she ever again get control over her tears? It
seemed like every little thing made her cry now. "I must look a
mess."

"No, you look beautiful. You'll always look beautiful to me."

"Even when I'm old?"

"Especially when you're old. If I already love you this much,
I can't imagine how much I'm gonna love you after spending
our lives together."

"Well, the good news is Mr. Barrera said you should get the
chance. He cleaned up the wound while you were out. He said
the main thing to watch for now is infection."

"Don't worry, Katie. It's gonna take more than a few bullets to kill me." He reached out and put one of his hands on top of hers. "I got too much to live for."

"Do you really think everything's going to be okay?"

"Heck yeah, it's gonna be okay. It's gonna be more than okay. I promise." He blinked up at her and gave her hand a squeeze. "Katie Quinn, will you marry me?"

She laughed, and here came the tears again. "Don't josh me like that, Lonnie."

"Who's joshing? I'm dead serious, Katie. I love you, and I want you to be my wife."

Katie gasped. Fear skewered her happiness.

"What is it?" Lonnie asked.

She got up and went to the wall and looked out the window, trying not to frame herself in the glass. "Two men in the yard. Strangers, with guns. Coming this way."

She heard the bed move, turned, and saw to her great horror that Lonnie was getting to his feet.

"Lonnie, what are you doing?"

"I'm going out there." He hobbled toward the door.

"You're hurt bad."

"I'm going out anyway. If these boys mean you harm," he said, wincing as he lifted his gun belt from beside the door, "I'd best get the drop on 'em."

"But Lonnie, your leg is broken—"

"Guess I'll hop, then." He grinned through the pain, not even a flicker of fear showing on his pale face.

And then, to her terror, he went out the door.

CHAPTER 51

Nora was sitting at the kitchen table with the Bible open when the door swung open and banged into the wall and a grinning Cyrus Undergrove came striding into the room.

He pointed his pistol at her and sneered with triumph. "Thought you got away, huh, sweetie?"

She merely stared, horror stricken. Then, coming to her senses, she slipped a hand under the table, meaning to draw the derringer.

"Oh no you don't," Undergrove said. "Get those hands where I can see them, or I swear I'll kill you."

Nora lifted her hands.

"That's more like it. You already shot me once. See what you did to my ear? Hurts like a day-old dog bite."

"Why are you here?"

"I came back for you, sugar dumpling. Didn't even hear me coming, did you?" Grinning, he held up a foot clad only in a filthy sock full of holes. "Took off my boots and snuck up injun style. Now, you're mine. I'm gonna use you to get the drop on that bounty hunter husband of yours, then I'm taking you to Mexico with me."

Nora laughed. She couldn't help it. "And here I thought you were just going to kill me. You think you're going to get the drop on Justice? Oh, you stupid man. Oh, you stupid, dead, dead man."

Undergrove took a step forward, his stubbled lip peeling back from his big teeth in a feral snarl. "We get to Mexico, I'm gonna teach you some manners, you—"

Out by the guesthouse, gunfire erupted, what sounded to a terrified Nora like numerous pistols all firing at once.

"Katie!"

CHAPTER 52

W hile Cyrus was still pulling his boots off, Slick worked his way slowly along the riverbank, looking for signs of the kid or his horse or that shaggy mutt that had been trotting along behind him.

He felt like a fool. What kind of work was this, anyway?

In his mind, he flashed back six months to when his father lay dying on the ground, plugged by his own son after an argument over checkers of all things.

He could still hear his mother crying in the doorway, still hear his father growling curses at him, telling him he'd never amount to anything, telling him he was dumb and lazy and a coward at heart.

And he could still hear the roar of the gun when he'd pulled the trigger again, silencing his father forever.

It was the first time he'd used a gun out of anger.

Then he'd run. A week later at a card table in El Paso, a man had rightfully accused him of cheating at cards, and he'd used the gun again, killing the man who couldn't pull his shooting iron in time.

A witness said, "Boy's slick. Never saw nobody so slick."

That's how Donnie Reese became the famous Wild West outlaw known as Slick.

Once he'd latched onto the notion of becoming a famous outlaw, he used it to cover the hole in his soul the way you laid boards over an old well.

When he shot another man in San Angelo, it was as much to silence his father's voice as it was anything against the man he killed.

Wouldn't amount to anything, huh?

Well, he'd just show his dad. He'd become the most famous outlaw in the whole West.

Since then, life had been mighty wild, especially after he met Cyrus and started robbing banks with the gang.

But of late, this life had lost some of its luster, and he'd been thinking of hanging up his guns, heading farther west, and maybe starting a new life under yet another name.

Yes, he'd thought these things, but here he was, hunting some little squirt through the scrub.

Some outlaw he was turning out to be.

And then, all of a sudden, he saw the kid.

The boy was on foot, maybe a hundred feet away, standing in front of a screen of heavy brush, staring at Slick with a look of terror.

Where was his horse? Where was the rifle? Where was that shaggy dog?

"Hey," Slick called, trying to sound friendly. He was glad

he'd left his Colt holstered. He raised a hand. "Hey, kid. Come here."

The kid plunged into the brush like a jackrabbit.

Cursing, Slick drew his pistol and ran.

Reaching the wall of scrub, he called out to the kid again.

There was no response.

He listened hard, trying to hear any movement in there, but heard only his own labored breathing, the gurgling of the river, and a low rumbling sound he couldn't identify.

Was that the kid? Was he crying his little eyes out and muffling it with a sleeve, the way Slick himself had done so many times during his own rocky childhood?

Suddenly, he wished he'd just stuck with the Bannerman twins. Or, instead of coming after this kid, just cut loose and ridden south as fast as he could.

But it was too late for all that. Now, he had to get that kid. If he didn't, Cyrus would be mad. And beyond Cyrus, he had to think of that bounty hunter, the kid's dad. He needed this kid as a bargaining chip.

"You don't come out here and be friendly," Slick hollered into the thick tangle, "I'm gonna be forced to shoot up that scrub, kid."

Silence.

"Don't matter to me," Slick told him. "I get paid either way, dead or alive, just like your daddy."

More silence.

He stepped forward and pushed at the scrub with his muzzle, craning his neck, looking for a flash of blond hair.

He didn't want to go in that thick brush chasing some snot-nosed kid, but he knew Cyrus would be mad if he made good on his threat and killed the boy.

"You want to live, kid, come on out. Now."

Silence.

What was wrong with this boy? Most kids, you talked that way to them, they'd come a running.

But this one must have ice water in his veins because he was just sitting tight, not making a peep.

Out of nowhere, Slick got the goosebumps.

Some outlaw you're shaping up to be, he chastised himself. Getting spooked by a little kid.

He skirted the brush, moving down the bank toward the river, and smiled.

There was the horse. And hallelujah, there was the rifle, still sitting in the boot.

He laughed as relief came flooding in.

Approaching the horse, he had a new, better idea.

"All right, little buddy. I hate to do it, but you leave me no choice. If you don't come out here right now, I'm gonna shoot your horse."

He stuck his head into the brush, looking for the boy. "Hear me, kid? You got to the count of three to show yourself, or I'm gonna kill your animal. One, two…"

The low rumbling sound he'd been hearing swelled into a growl, and a multicolored blur burst from the scrub.

Slick had just enough time to register the feral eyes and sharp, white teeth before the wild thing pounded into him.

A wolf, he thought as he toppled, the world exploding in shock and pain, and he tried to scream, but you can't scream when your throat's been ripped out.

CHAPTER 53

Justice hammered down the road past the outlaws' horses, knowing it might all be a trap, that they might be waiting to shoot him out of the saddle.

But there was no time for caution because he'd heard gunshots.

He pounded into the yard, hopped down, and filled his hands with Colts.

And at that very moment, a smiling Cyrus Undergrove came out of the house, propelling Nora before him and keeping the muzzle of his pistol to her head.

"Well, if it ain't the famous bounty hunter," Cyrus said. He was giddy, bubbling over with confidence. "What are you gonna do, huh? You can't shoot me, or I'll pull the trigger. Even if you're as fast as they say, you know dying men twitch. One little jerk of my finger, and it's bye-bye for your pretty wife. Is that what you want, Bullard?"

"No, it's not," Justice said. It would be such a simple thing, pulling the trigger and killing him, but he couldn't do it. He knew Undergrove spoke the truth.

Justice could see no way out.

"Just shoot him, Justice," Nora said. Her voice was steady, and her face was curiously calm. "Just shoot him, and if anything happens to me, you and I will be reunited in heaven."

Cyrus ignored her, grinning at Justice. "What do you want more, the money or your woman?"

Behind him, down low to the ground, something was coming out of Nora's flowers. Two somethings, in fact.

"Speak up," Cyrus shouted. "What do you say, Bullard?"

Justice, seeing the multicolored forms slinking forward, smiled. "I say… sic 'em, boys!"

"Huh?"

The hulking pups attacked without hesitation, for they were the sons of Rafer, the very wolfdog who had twice killed men in defense of his family.

The pups were too small to tear out the throat of the man hurting Eli's mother and barking at their alpha, but they sunk their small, sharp teeth into the man's legs with unbridled ferocity. One latched onto his Achilles tendon, tearing it from the ankle. The other plunged his needle teeth into the soft spot behind Cyrus's knee.

Cyrus screamed a high, keening, desperate squeal and jerked involuntarily, his muzzle swinging away from Nora's temple. Justice shot him between the eyes.

Nora stepped away as the corpse dropped to the ground, where it was further savaged by the determined pups.

Rafer must be off with Eli, Justice figured. The dog had

probably snarled when the pups tried to follow, which left them hiding in the flowers. Praise God for that.

Justice rushed to Nora.

But she pushed past him, wiping blood from her face as she ran toward the guesthouse, eyes bulging with terror she hadn't shown at gunpoint. "Katie!" she gasped. "Oh, Justice, I heard a lot of gunshots. Katie!"

Justice hurtled toward the guesthouse, racing past Nora. He had become a force of fury, ready to kill anyone and everyone who dared to harm the daughter he loved so very, very much.

Coming around the corner, he saw two dead men lying on the ground.

And there, kneeling just outside the doorway, was Katie.

She sobbed, rocking back and forth, cradling the limp body of the boy with long, golden hair.

CHAPTER 54

"Oh, how I prayed," Katie said, later that evening after the town surgeon, Alfredo Barrera, departed. She sat in a chair beside the bed, her fingertips stroking Lonnie's blond locks. "I thought you were dead."

Lonnie's eyes stared up from his pale face with great intensity. "Me, die? Nah, I told you... I got too much to live for."

His voice was weak, which made sense, given how much trauma he had endured and how much blood he had lost.

"I'm just so thankful you're okay," Katie said.

"Truth be told, I've been okayer."

She laughed. "You know what I mean, silly. I'm just grateful you survived. Praise God!"

He nodded at that.

The door opened.

Katie jumped involuntarily but saw it was only Pa, not more attackers.

Pa stood there in the doorway for a moment, stern-faced, his hard, green eyes looking back and forth between them.

Then he spoke to Lonnie. "You're awake."

"Yes, sir."

Pa nodded. All was silent for a few seconds.

Katie's heart pounded as her father studied the man she loved.

What was he going to say?

"Let me get this straight," Pa said. "You got up, wounded as you were, gunned down two bad men despite getting plugged again, then hobbled back to check on Katie before collapsing?"

"Yes, sir. Except I don't really remember the last part. I just remember the fight, knowing they were dead, then worrying about Katie. I don't remember the rest, you know, passing out and all."

"That's just how it happened," Katie said, sitting up a little straighter, her love for Lonnie burning bright.

Pa nodded, still staring at Lonnie, but said nothing for another moment.

Katie's heart pounded harder. She knew this was it, knew Pa was about to say something that would change everything forever.

Finally, he said, "Well, I don't guess anybody with the sand to get up on a broken leg and fight is going to give up on the girl he loves, is he?"

"No, sir," Lonnie said, holding her father's gaze. "Not ever."

Pa looked at him for another silent moment, his eyes thoughtful. Then he nodded. "You'll do to ride the river with."

Then her father, the man called Justice, turned and went out the door, leaving the two of them alone.

A lump rose in Katie's throat, and happy tears blurred her vision.

Lonnie blinked up at her, confused by her tears and, because he'd grown up in the desert, also confused about Justice's words. "Ride the river? Is your pa mad at me?"

Katie laughed, shaking her head. "No, Lonnie. Not at all. Pa has his ways. You might even say he's a touch odd. But he just gave you the highest compliment he's ever given anyone in his life."

"Oh," Lonnie said. "He sure didn't look happy."

Katie laughed again, her heart bursting with love for Lonnie and her father. "When Pa speaks like that, smile or no smile, it's more than a compliment. It's a promise. And he's a man who keeps his promises, always and forever."

Lonnie's big hand closed over hers, and he stared up at her with love burning in his eyes. "I am the same sort of man, Katie. I will always keep my promises."

"I know you will, Lonnie," Katie said, "And so will I."

She brushed his golden locks aside, leaned forward, and touched her lips to his, kissing him for the first time. "Here's to keeping our promises."

———

THANK YOU FOR READING *JUSTICE RIDES AGAIN*.

Next up is Heck & Hope #2, Heck's Valley.

If you enjoyed this story, please be a friend and leave a review. When you leave even a short review, you just bought my family dinner, because Amazon will show the book to more people. I sure would appreciate your help.

If you enjoyed the book but don't have time to review, please consider leaving a 5-star rating. It's quick and simple and helps me get this new series off the ground.

To hear about new releases, special sales, and giveaways, join my reader list.

Once more, thanks for reading. I hope our paths cross again. And with holidays fast approaching, I wish you and yours good health, a wonderful Thanksgiving, and a blessed Christmas.

Until then, don't approach a bull from the front, a horse from the rear, or a fool from any direction.

ABOUT THE AUTHOR

I was born six months before man landed on the moon and lucky enough to grow up in the country, where my family lived largely off the land.

When I wasn't fishing, exploring the woods, or weeding the garden, I devoured comic books like *Two-Gun Kid* and *The Rawhide Kid* before moving on to the exciting adventure stories of Jack London and Louis L'Amour.

Our black-and-white TV only got three channels, though you could lose one and pick up another if you went outside and messed with the antenna. On its grainy screen, we watched *Gunsmoke*, *Bonanza*, and movies starring John Wayne and Clint Eastwood.

Now a husband and father, I love traveling the West and reading history and fiction alike. My favorite authors are Louis L'Amour, Elmore Leonard, C.J. Petit, and R.O. Lane.

ALSO BY JOHN DEACON

John's Amazon author page has all of his books in various formats: Kindle, paperback, hardcover, and audiobook.

A Man Called Justice (Silent Justice #1)

Justice Returns (Silent Justice #2)

Final Justice (Silent Justice #3)

Justice Rides Again (Silent Justice #4)

Destitution

Heck's Journey (Heck & Hope #1)

Heck's Valley (Heck & Hope #2)

Heck's Gold (Heck & Hope #3)

Heck's Gamble (Heck & Hope #4)

Heck's Stand (Heck & Hope #5)

Lobo (The Lobo Trilogy #1)

Lobo 2 (The Lobo Trilogy #2)

Lobo 3 (The Lobo Trilogy #3)

The Provider (The Provider Saga #1)

The Provider 2 (The Provider Saga #2)

Printed in Dunstable, United Kingdom

63749364R00150